S0-AUY-777

"Sally… May I call you Sally?" he asked politely, then went on, "You are a beautiful young woman. Your father must be a very proud man."

Overblown words of flattery from a man whose dark eyes contained a sexually explicit invitation did not impress her. Her mother was her only concern.

Straightening her slender shoulders, she held out her hand politely. "Nice to meet you," she said flatly.

Zac Delucca did not miss the flash of distaste in her brilliant blue eyes as he finally let go of her hand.

Her voice was low and ever so slightly husky. Her brilliant blue eyes had been cool as she glanced up at him and swiftly back to her father. Never had a woman so instantly dismissed him. Yet this beauty had done it twice. Her indifference rankled, and he was all the more determined to make her aware of him….

Welcome to the April 2010 collection of fabulous Presents stories for your indulgence!

About to lose his kingdom, Xavian will bed his new queen, but could she be his undoing? Find out in the first installment of our sizzling DARK-HEARTED DESERT MEN miniseries, *Wedlocked: Banished Sheikh, Untouched Queen* by Carol Marinelli. They're devastating, dark-hearted and looking for brides!

Why not enjoy two fabulous stories in one with *Her Mediterranean Playboy* by exciting authors Melanie Milburne and Kate Hewitt. Be seduced under the Mediterranean sun, where wild playboys tame their mistresses!

Isobel has never forgotten the night Brazilian millionaire Alejandro Cabral took her innocence, but when he discovers she had his daughter, he'll stop at nothing to claim her again in *The Brazilian Millionaire's Love-Child* by author Anne Mather.

Why not unwind with a sexy story of seduction and glamour—Xavier DeVasquez will have innocent Romy slipping between his sheets one more time in Helen Bianchin's *Bride, Bought and Paid For.* Sally must become Zac's mistress on demand or risk ruin in Jacqueline Baird's *Untamed Italian, Blackmailed Innocent!* And billionaire Lorenzo Valente vows to have his wedding night in *The Blackmail Baby* by Natalie Rivers.

Look out for the next tantalizing installment of DARK-HEARTED DESERT MEN in May with Jennie Lucas's *Tamed: The Barbarian King!*

The glamour, the excitement, the intensity just keep getting better!

Jacqueline Baird

UNTAMED ITALIAN, BLACKMAILED INNOCENT

HARLEQUIN®

TORONTO • NEW YORK • LONDON
AMSTERDAM • PARIS • SYDNEY • HAMBURG
STOCKHOLM • ATHENS • TOKYO • MILAN • MADRID
PRAGUE • WARSAW • BUDAPEST • AUCKLAND

If you purchased this book without a cover you should be aware
that this book is stolen property. It was reported as "unsold and
destroyed" to the publisher, and neither the author nor the
publisher has received any payment for this "stripped book."

Recycling programs
for this product may
not exist in your area.

ISBN-13: 978-0-373-23675-6

UNTAMED ITALIAN, BLACKMAILED INNOCENT

First North American Publication 2010.

Copyright © 2010 by Jacqueline Baird.

All rights reserved. Except for use in any review, the reproduction or
utilization of this work in whole or in part in any form by any electronic,
mechanical or other means, now known or hereafter invented, including
xerography, photocopying and recording, or in any information storage
or retrieval system, is forbidden without the written permission of the
publisher, Harlequin Enterprises Limited, 225 Duncan Mill Road,
Don Mills, Ontario M3B 3K9, Canada.

This is a work of fiction. Names, characters, places and incidents are
either the product of the author's imagination or are used fictitiously,
and any resemblance to actual persons, living or dead, business
establishments, events or locales is entirely coincidental.

This edition published by arrangement with Harlequin Books S.A.

® and TM are trademarks of the publisher. Trademarks indicated with
® are registered in the United States Patent and Trademark Office, the
Canadian Trade Marks Office and in other countries.

www.eHarlequin.com

Printed in U.S.A.

All about the author...
Jacqueline Baird

JACQUELINE BAIRD was born and raised in Northumbria, U.K. She met her husband when she was eighteen. Eight years later, after many adventures around the world, she came home and married him. They still live in Northumbria and now have two grown-up sons.

Jacqueline's number-one passion is writing. She has always been an avid reader and she had her first success as a writer at the age of eleven, when she won first prize in the Nature Diary of the Year competition at school. But she always felt a little guilty because her diary was more fiction than fact.

She always loved romance novels and when her sons went to school all day, she thought she would try writing one. She's been writing for the Harlequin Presents® line ever since, and she still gets a thrill every time a new book is published.

When Jacqueline is not busy writing, she likes to spend her time traveling, reading and playing cards. She was a keen sailor until a knee injury ended her sailing days, but she still enjoys swimming in the sea when the weather allows.

She visits a gym three times a week and has made the surprising discovery that she gets some good ideas while doing the mind-numbingly boring exercises on the cycling and weight machines.

CHAPTER ONE

ZAC DELUCCA stepped out of the chauffeur-driven limousine and glanced up at the four-storeyed Georgian-style building in front of him: the head office of Westwold Components, a company he had finally acquired two weeks ago. He had left Raffe, his top man, in charge of the changeover, so he had not expected to be needed in London in June, and he was not pleased....

He was ruggedly attractive, with black hair and shrewd dark eyes, and the navy silk and mohair suit he wore was a testament to the expertise of his tailor. The jacket stretched taut across shoulders as wide as a barn door, and at six feet five he was a powerful, impressive figure of a man in every respect. Not a man anyone could overlook, though the fierce frown at present marring his bold features would scare all but the bravest into glancing the other way.

Orphaned at a year old by the tragic death of his

young parents in a car crash, Zac Delucca had spent his early years in a children's home in Rome. He had left at fifteen, with nothing but the clothes he stood up in and a burning ambition to become a success in life.

Tall, and looking older than his years, he had by sheer guts, determination and keen intelligence dragged himself up from the gutter that beckoned. He had studied by day and used his physical strength in the testosterone-fuelled world of the fighting game at night to earn money and build up a stake to set up his own company: Delucca Holdings.

He had fought masked, under an assumed name, because he'd had total belief in his ability, mentally and physically, to be a winner in life. From a young age he had known he was destined to succeed on a worldwide scale…never mind in a canvas ring…

His first purchase at the age of twenty had been a rundown farm in southern Italy that had included three cottages, a large farmhouse and a thousand acres of neglected land. A few weeks later the government had bought a chunk of the acreage to build a new runway to expand a local airport for the increasing tourist trade.

Some people said he'd had inside information. He had said nothing and recouped the money he had invested and more besides. He'd converted the farm house, which was situated on the coast at the southernmost tip of Italy, with stunning views over the sea, and kept it for his own use.

The remaining land had included an overgrown olive grove he had tried to cultivate himself, but he had quickly realised agriculture was not for him and finally hired an expert in the field to restore, enlarge and manage the farm, while converting the cottages for the staff. Eventually he'd marketed the produce as Delucca Extra Fine Virgin Olive Oil, and Delucca Oil was today the choice of the connoisseur and priced accordingly...

It was the first business Zac had bought and kept.

Now, fifteen years later, Delucca Holdings was an international conglomerate that owned a vast array of companies, including mines, manufacturers, properties and oil of the petroleum variety as well as from the olive tree. Nothing was out of Delucca's grasp.

Ruthless, arrogant, and merciless were some of the terms used by his enemies, but none in the business world friend or enemy could deny he was a financial wizard, and basically honest... A master of the universe who went after what he wanted and always succeeded.

'Are you sure about this, Raffe?' Zac demanded of the man who had exited the car to join him on the pavement.

Raffe Costa was his right-hand man and his friend.

They had met over a decade ago, when Zac had applied for funding for a deal from a bank in Naples, where Raffe had been working in the commercial loan office. The pair had hit it off immediately, and two years later Raffe had joined Zac's swiftly expanding company as an accountant-cum-PA. The title was not important. Zac trusted him completely, and knew him to be shrewd and rarely wrong.

'Sure…?' Raffe responded slowly. 'No, I am not absolutely sure, but enough to want you to check it out,' he qualified as they walked towards the entrance. 'It wasn't noticed in the due diligence we conducted before buying, because the siphoning off of funds—if that is what it is—has been done very cleverly, and been deeply hidden in the accounts for years.'

'You'd better be right. Because I had plans to take a holiday, and I did not intend it to be in London,' Zac said dryly, flicking his friend a glance as they entered the building. 'I had a hot climate and a hot woman in mind.'

Zac Delucca was not a happy man. He had no trouble in thinking on several levels at the same time, and right now, while smiling at the security guard as Raffe introduced him, another part of his mind was wondering how quickly—if Raffe's suspicions were correct—he could sort out the problem and leave…

He had, after months of prolonged negotiation, finalised this deal. Coincidentally it had been the following morning, standing in the shower, that he realised he had been celibate for almost a year. Ten months since he had parted with his last lady, because she was becoming too proprietorial and the *M* word had surfaced more than once.

Amazed at his own restraint, he had swiftly decided to rectify the situation by arranging a couple of dates with a rather striking model from Milan. He had planned to take her out on his yacht for the day and make her his mistress. If they proved to be compatible he had actually considered breaking the habit of a lifetime and allowing her to accompany him on a cruise around the Caribbean for a few weeks.

He had never taken more than a week's holiday in years, but just lately he'd found himself questioning if work was the be-all and end-all of life. Unusual for him. He was not usually given to bouts of introspection and immediately he had decided to do something about it—hence Lisa the Milan model…

Unfortunately, the call last night from Raffe, voicing some concern over the recent acquisition of Westwold Components, looked like scuppering his plan.

He signed the log-in book where the security guard indicated—a formality, but no doubt the man wanted to impress—and was then introduced to the receptionist: Melanie.

'I'm sure Mr Costa will have told you,' the girl simpered, while hanging on to Zac's hand like a leech. 'We are all really happy to become part of Delucca Holdings, and if there is anything I personally can do…' The busty blonde fluttered her eyelashes at him. 'Just ask.'

The woman gushed and pouted at the same time, which was quite a feat, Zac thought cynically.

'Thank you,' he replied smoothly, and, disentangling his hand from the receptionist's grasp, he turned. 'Come on, Raffe, let's get—' And he stopped, his dark eyes instinctively flaring in primitive masculine appreciation of the woman walking into the building.

'Exquisite,' he murmured under his breath, his stunned gaze roaming over her. She had the face of an angel, and a body to tempt any man with blood in his veins…

Big, misty-blue eyes, pale, almost translucent skin, a small nose and a wide mouth with full lips that begged to be kissed. Long ruby-red hair fell in soft curls around her slender shoulders, and the elegant white obviously designer dress she wore caressed every curve of her slender body. Sleeveless, with a low square neck and a broad white belt circling her tiny waist, it accentuated her high full breasts.

She looked bridal… The unbidden thought flashed in his mind. But the evocative tap of high-heeled shoes on the marble floor knocked it straight out as his gaze lowered to where the hem of the skirt ended on her knees. The red stiletto sandals she wore screamed sex.

His heart almost stopped. She had legs to die for… A mental image of them clamped around his waist had his body hardening instantly.

'Who is that?' he demanded of Raffe.

'I have no idea, but she is gorgeous.'

Zac looked at his friend and saw he was watching the girl as she drew nearer. He had to bite his lip to stop himself saying, *Take your eyes off her. She is mine.*

In that instant he came to a decision. Admittedly she was not his usual type. Tall, elegant brunettes had been his preference up until now. This woman was average height, with that long, red hair, but for some inexplicable reason he wanted her with a hunger he had not felt in a long time. He decided he was going to have her…

His firm lips parted in a loaded smile aimed directly at her, but amazingly the girl walked straight past him with a dismissive shake of her head…

Sally Paxton strode across the foyer of Westwold Components, determination in every step. She flicked a glance at the group of people at the reception desk and caught a brilliant smile from the tallest man in the group. Her heart missed a beat and she felt her shoulders stiffen with tension. She had to appear confident, as if she belonged here. Maybe he was someone she should recognise… She gave a brief nod of her head in acknowledgment.

Sally Paxton was a woman on a mission…and nothing and no one was going to stop her…

Her blue eyes fixed with a determined light on the two elevators situated to the rear of the elegant foyer. One elevator she knew was for general use; the other—the one she wanted—went directly to the top floor, where her father's office was situated.

Zac Delucca, for the first time in his adult life, had been virtually overlooked by a woman, and for a moment it left him dumbfounded.

Recovering, he demanded of the receptionist, 'Who is that girl, and what department does she work in?'

'I don't know. I've never seen her before.'

'Security,' he said, alerting the guard standing nearby, but he was already calling out.

'Stop, miss, you have to sign in!'

Sally stopped in front of the elevator and jabbed at the button, lost in her own angry thoughts. The one and only time she had visited her dad's London office had been over seven years ago. She had been eighteen and had called in unannounced one Wednesday afternoon, after watching her beloved mother open a birthday card from her husband that morning.

Sally had been hoping to persuade her dad to return with her that evening to their home in Bournemouth, rather than waiting until the weekend. It was her mum's birthday, for heaven's sake... At least he had remembered to post a card... But as her mother had recently been discharged from hospital after a mastectomy, Sally had been determined to make him see that his wife needed his support.

The success of the surprise dinner party Sally had planned for the evening had depended on her father's presence.

Her lips tightened in disgust, and briefly she closed her eyes. Even now the scene that had met her eyes was still scorched into her brain, and made her simmer with rage...

Nigel Paxton's secretary had not been in the outer office, so Sally had knocked on her father's door. When no one had answered she had opened it and walked in.

It had not been a pretty sight... There was her dad, leaning over his desk with his half-naked secretary, half his age, sprawled across the desk beneath him.

No wonder they hadn't heard her knock…

Her father…the slick seducer…the serial adulterer…the slimy lying toad…the man her mother loved and thought could do no wrong—the man Sally had slowly grown to despise.

The elevator arrived and she stepped in and pressed the button. Leaning back against the wall, she closed her eyes.

As a young child she supposed she had loved her father, even though he hadn't been around a lot. Their home in Bournemouth had been a large detached Victorian house overlooking the sea. But her father, as chief accountant for Westwolds Components, was based in the London headquarters of the company, and kept a studio apartment in the city where he stayed during the week.

As an idealistic teenager, anti-war of any kind, she had been horrified when she'd realised the firm her dad worked for manufactured essential parts for weapons. She had announced that it was morally wrong to work in the arms industry, and he had told her she was a silly girl, and to stick to looking good and leave the running of the world to men.

To call him a male chauvinist pig was to insult pigs! Dark haired, handsome and charming to those who did not know him, her father was at the top of his game in the accountancy stakes—but in Sally's book he was a spineless apology for a man.

Well, today he was going to hear just what she thought of him—yet again, and demand he accompany her to visit her mother in the private nursing home in Devon that had been her mum's home for almost two years.

It was over six weeks since her father had shown his face, and she blinked tears from her eyes as she pictured again the look on her mum's face every time Sally arrived to visit. The gleam of hope that faded as she realised her latest visitor was not her husband yet again. Sally's excuse for her dad that 'pressure of work' kept him in London was wearing very thin.

Her mother knew about his affairs, because Sally at eighteen had blurted out what she had seen. And her mother had admitted she had always known about her husband's other women—in the *plural*!

Sally had been horrified when her mother had actually made excuses for him. Explaining how it was difficult for him as a virile man, because she had not been a very able wife in the bedroom department for quite some time even before she had been diagnosed with breast cancer, and that he was a good and generous husband and father and she loved him.

Nothing Sally said had affected her mother's opinion or her love for her husband, and, not wanting to upset her mother, she had been forced to drop the subject.

As for her father—she'd told him exactly what she thought of him, and he had simply responded with the usual: that she was a silly girl who knew nothing of the wants and needs of adults, and that she should mind her own business and concentrate on her studies, because he was paying enough for them…

Immediately, she had wanted to give up her place at Exeter University, where she'd been in her first year studying Ancient History, but her mother would not hear of it. Reluctantly, Sally had to agree, but she could barely bring herself to be civil to her father when he did occasionally return home the same weekend as her.

As it happened, her mother had been right to insist on her continuing her education, because her mum had recovered from the breast cancer remarkably well. Sally had watched her slowly begin to grow in confidence and hope as test after test had come back with positive results.

When her mum had reached the five-year point and still been in the clear she had told Sally it was time for her to spread her wings a little and strike out on her own. After graduating Sally had initially worked at a small local museum near home. But after her mother's encouragement she had applied and secured a job as a researcher at the British Museum in London.

Sally had loved her new job—and the fully furnished one-bedroom apartment she had rented over a bakery in the city. For the first six months life had been good. Her mum had been well, and had occasionally visited her in London. Sally had gone home most weekends, and, excluding her dad, the future had looked rosy. Then the horrendous tragedy of her mum's accident had destroyed their fragile happiness.

Even now Sally could not get her head around how fate could be so cruel… She shook her head as a huge black cloud of sadness enveloped her. It was so unfair. After five years her mum had virtually recovered from the cancer. Only to be knocked down by a car as she walked out behind the bus she had taken to the centre of Bournemouth to shop. After months of treatment she had been left a paraplegic, with no hope of further improvement.

Now every weekend Sally travelled down to Devon, where she stayed in a small hotel near the nursing home so she could spend as much time with her mother as possible. Last Saturday evening Sally had been sitting with her mother and had watched her face light up at the sound of her husband's voice on the telephone, had seen in her eyes the pain and sadness she'd tried to hide as she replaced the receiver, and had listened with growing anger as her mother repeated the conversation.

Apparently her father had called to tell her he

could not make it on Sunday, nor the next
weekend… His excuse was that with the takeover
of the company by the Italian firm Delucca
Holdings, he was up to his ears in work.

Sally opened her eyes and took a deep breath.
She needed to calm down, and she needed to plan
what she was going to say to her father. Yelling at
him would be futile. For her mother's sake she
needed him to go to the nursing home with her
willingly, for once in his selfish life, to act the part
of loving husband.

God knew it wasn't as if he was going to have
to do it for long… If the consultant was to be
believed, her mother's life expectancy was limited.

On her last visit the doctor had called Sally into
his consulting room and informed her that her
mother's heart was weakened beyond repair,
probably as a result of the cancer treatment she had
undergone combined with the accident that had
followed. He was sorry, but there was nothing more
that could be done, and in his opinion her mother
had maybe a year at best. But in reality she could
go at any time.

The doors opened and Sally exited the
elevator. Her dad's office was at the far end of the
corridor, and, squaring her shoulders, she tightened her grip on her red clutch purse and made
straight for his door.

* * *

Zac Delucca crossed to where the security guard stood, pressing the button for the elevator.

'Sorry, sir, she got away. But this elevator only goes to the top floor, where the boardroom and Mr Costa's office is situated. The only other office is Mr Paxton's, the company accountant, but that wasn't his girlfriend—secretary,' he quickly corrected himself. 'Maybe the lady is looking for you?' he suggested, trying to sound positive after having failed in his duty to register all visitors.

So the accountant was having an affair... Zac filed the information away. 'Do not worry, Joe,' he said, glancing at the name tag on his uniform. 'You were distracted—and if what you say is true the lady is not going anywhere. I suggest you get back to you desk.'

The elevator doors glided open, and Zac and Raffe entered.

'Is the lady *likely* to be looking for you?' Raffe asked with a grin. 'Or should I say chasing?'

'I should be so lucky,' Zac drawled, though it was a common occurrence for women to chase him. He was an incredibly wealthy man and, as one reporter had once written, with his kind of wealth, good looks and height—a broken nose notwithstanding—he was a magnet for women the world over. Not that he thought of himself as such...

Concentrating on the task at hand, he asked, 'It

is the accountant whom you suspect of fraud, is it not, Raffe?'

'Yes.'

'I take it he is a married man?'

'Yes—married with one child, I believe.'

'And apparently this man has a mistress, and they do not come cheap. Your suspicions are looking well founded, Raffe.'

Sally walked straight into her father's office and stopped. He was sitting behind his desk, his head in his hands, a picture of misery. Maybe she had misjudged him... Maybe he was more upset over his wife's diagnosis than he showed.

'Dad?' she called softly, and he lifted his head.

'Oh, it's you.' He straightened up, frowning. 'What are you doing here? No, don't tell me.' He raised his hand. 'You are on a holier-than-thou mission and want me to go and visit your mum, right?'

He wasn't upset. He was the same selfish bastard he had always been.

'Silly me.' Sally shook her head in disgust. 'For a moment there I thought you were thinking of your wife...' She glanced around the large room and through the open door to the secretary's office beyond, which was empty, and then back to her dad.

'Well, I have had enough of your lies and deceit,

and for once in your life you are going to do the decent thing and come with me tonight.'

'Not now, darling,' he snapped, and stood up, straightening his tie.

Zac Delucca had heard the woman's demand that Paxton go with her as he entered the office, and he did not miss the *darling*, or the sardonic curl of the woman's lips as she responded.

'What's the matter? Your latest Girl Friday deserted you? And I use the word *girl* deliberately,' Sally goaded. And she must have hit the nail on the head as the colour seemed to drain from her dad's face. Then she realised he was looking straight past her. The smile on his face did not reach the eyes that for an instant flickered with fear, quickly masked.

Inexplicably, Sally shivered, despite the slight stuffiness of the office on the hot summer's day, and she felt the hairs on the back of her neck stand on end. Someone else had entered the room, probably his secretary, and she was now shooting daggers at her back, having overheard her comment. Not that Sally gave a damn about upsetting her dad's latest mistress…

'Mr Costa, I was not expecting you back again so soon.'

Sally stiffened as her dad spoke and then stepped forward, ignoring her. Then she heard the Costa man introduce a Signor Delucca.

'Mr Delucca, this is an unexpected pleasure. I am delighted to meet you.'

Her father's hearty greeting rang a little false to Sally. She knew every intonation of his voice, and he did not sound delighted. She certainly was not. His secretary she could handle, but she stiffened as she recognised the name Delucca.

After her father had stated the man was taking over the company Sally had read an article about him in the business section of a newspaper. He was an Italian tycoon, incredibly wealthy, and renowned as the takeover king. His latest acquisition was Westwold. In a footnote to the article, it said that apparently he kept his private life very private, but it was known that he had escorted numerous statuesque models in his time.

Unbelievable… Sally fumed silently. For years she had for her mum's benefit kept the peace with her father, even if it had been mostly by ignoring him. But today, for the first time in years, she had decided to challenge him and demand he cut out the lies and the girlfriend for the weekend and do the right thing by his wife. Instead, for once it seemed he might have been telling the truth. The new owner Delucca was here. Perhaps her dad did intend working the weekend…

But not if she could help it…

CHAPTER TWO

ZAC DELUCCA walked forward and briefly shook the hand Nigel Paxton held out to him. 'The pleasure is mine,' he said suavely, and, turning, shifted his attention to the stunning woman.

He studied her intently for a long moment. Her gaze was fixed on Paxton and never wavered. She did not even glance at Zac, and he was intrigued. Could this gorgeous woman actually be Paxton's lover? Or maybe, by the sound of the conversation he had overheard, a discarded lover? Both scenarios he found very hard to believe. Firstly, she was too young for Paxton, and secondly, any man who had such a female in his bed would be a fool to let her go. With a face and figure like hers she could take her pick of the male population and probably did, he concluded as he noted the banked-down fire in her ice-blue eyes that to a man with his expert knowledge of women denoted a passionate nature.

'Sorry to intrude. I was not aware you had

company,' he continued, turning his attention back to the accountant—the possible thief, he reminded himself. 'You must introduce me to your charming friend, Paxton,' he commanded, and waited, his dark eyes once again roaming over the woman's lovely face and exquisite body.

Sally barely registered the stranger's smooth tones as her dad made the introduction.

'Oh, she is not my friend,' her father chuckled, and beamed down at her. He had got that right, she thought cynically. 'This is my daughter, Sally.'

She turned slightly and looked up, and up again, at a positive giant of a man—with black hair and black eyes, and no doubt a black heart, if his unashamed masculine scrutiny of her body was anything to go by.

'Sally… May I call you Sally?' he asked politely, then went on, 'You are a beautiful young woman. Your father must be a very proud man.'

Why did she get the feeling there was an underlying cynicism in his tone? Not that she cared. Overblown words of flattery from a man with a sexually explicit invitation in the dark eyes that met hers did not impress her, and she refused to be intimidated. Her mother was her only concern, and she shrugged off the unfamiliar tremor that slid down her spine.

Straightening her slender shoulders, she held out

her hand politely, and it was immediately engulfed in his much larger one. 'Nice to meet you,' she said flatly, and looked back at her father again. At the same time she attempted to slip her hand from Delucca's, but outrageously his thumb slowly stroked the length of her palm and her fingers before setting her free.

How predictable—another one like her dad, she thought bitterly.

Zac Delucca did not miss the flash of distaste in her brilliant blue eyes as he finally let go of her hand. Maybe caressing her palm had been a little juvenile, but he had been unable to resist the temptation to test the softness of her skin against his. For a moment he imagined the brush of every inch of her skin against his naked body, and had to fight to control the surge of arousal the thought induced.

He had definitely been too long without a woman, but now he knew it was not Lisa in Milan or any other woman he wanted. It was *this* woman he wanted, and he resolved to have her. He had no doubt he would succeed—he always did. It was simply a matter of negotiating the when and where, sooner rather than later, if his neglected libido had any say in the matter.

Her voice was low, and ever so slightly husky. Her brilliant blue eyes had been cool as she glanced up at him and swiftly back to her father. Never had a woman so instantly dismissed him. Usually *they* hung on to *his* hand… Yet this beauty had done it twice. Her indifference rankled, and he was all the more determined to make her aware of him…

He watched as her father introduced her to Raffe. She gave him an equally brief smile and turned back to her father yet again. But as she continued speaking, Zac sensed it was not so much that she was ignoring him, but that she was disappointed in her father for some reason. He noted the dark flush that stained the older man's face and he felt the tension between them.

Thinking fast, Sally spoke. 'I hope you don't mind, Mr Delucca,' she said without actually looking at the man, her hard blue eyes fixed on the reprobate that was her father. 'I called round to persuade my father to take me out to lunch. I am always telling him he works far too many hours. Isn't that right, Dad?' she prompted sweetly.

She did not want to reveal her mother's poor health to two virtual strangers, but she did need to get her dad by himself and extract a promise from him to go with her—if not tonight, then in the morning—to visit his wife. He was not fobbing her off again.

'Yes, but you are a little late. I had a sandwich earlier, as I am rather busy, and as you can see, Mr Delucca, the new owner of the company, has just arrived. I can't possibly take you to lunch today. Why don't you run along and I will ring you this evening?'

Next he would be patting her on the head, like the silly girl he thought she was, Sally thought angrily. She knew perfectly well he would not call her tonight. She knew every lying tone of his voice. But she also realised there was not much she could do about it. Not with two strange men standing listening to the exchange.

She stared at her father for a moment. He was smiling his usual charming smile, and yet there was something… She could hear the underlying strain in his voice. Whether it was because she had turned up or because of his new boss's presence she wasn't sure, but before she could decide she felt the brief brush of long male fingers on her forearm—apparently to get her attention. Involuntarily she tensed at the touch, and glanced up in surprise, her blue eyes clashing with black.

'Your father is right, Sally. He is going to be occupied for the rest of the day with Raffe, my accountant.'

For some inexplicable reason, Sally was paralysed by the dark eyes holding hers. They were not actually black, more a deep dark brown, with the faintest tinge of gold, and framed by the longest, thickest, sootiest eyelashes she had ever seen on a man.

What on earth was she doing? She tried to look away. Her mother was her only concern. But somehow her gaze lingered for a moment on his striking face. He wasn't handsome, she decided. At some time his nose had been broken, and had healed, leaving a slight bump, and above one arched black eyebrow there was an inch-long scar.

'But I could not possibly allow a young lady to lunch alone.'

Still studying his face, she was only half registering his words. Then with a jolt she swiftly lowered her gaze as she suddenly had a good idea where his statement was going. She glanced back up to see Delucca turn his attention to her dad.

'If you have no objection, Paxton, I will take your daughter to lunch. Raffe is more than capable of explaining the business we need to discuss, and I will see you later.'

Sally was too stunned by the turn of events to object immediately. Instead she glanced from one man to the other, and caught the hardest look pass between them, and then her father responded—at his jovial best.

'That is extremely kind of you, Mr Delucca. Problem solved. Sally, darling, Mr Delucca will take you to lunch—isn't that good of him?'

Sally looked from her dad up to the man towering over her, his dark eyes gleaming with sardonic

amusement and something more she did not want
to recognise. She shivered and did not bother to
answer her dad. Good…? There was nothing good
about this man. Of that she was sure…

Ten minutes later Sally was sitting in the back of
a limousine, Zac Delucca seated beside her, on her
way to a lunch she did not really want.

'Comfortable, Sally?'

'Fine,' she responded automatically. How the
hell had this happened? she asked herself for the
umpteenth time.

'The restaurant is about twenty minutes away—
a favourite of mine when I am in London.'

'Fine,' she murmured, rerunning in her head the
conversation in the office.

When she had finally found her voice she had
tried to get out of going to lunch with the excuse
that she wasn't that hungry and she was sure Mr
Delucca was far too busy to waste time with her.

Delucca had silkily stated that time was never
wasted with a beautiful woman. She had noted the
devilish humour in his dark eyes, and just known
he was laughing at her. He was the kind of man
who always won, and she had wanted to slap him.

He'd known that as well, she was sure.

Then there was her dad, who for some reason had
seemed very keen for her to go out with the man.

In fact, he had practically insisted. With the two of them ganging up on her, she'd never had a chance.

Still, how bad could it be? she asked herself. A quick meal and then she could leave Delucca at the restaurant and grab a cab home. She gazed out of the car window and idly wondered how they made the tinted glass that looked black from the outside of the car, but from the inside was clear, allowing her to see everything outside.

She felt the brush of a hard masculine thigh against her own and moved slightly. If Delucca was coming on to her he was wasting his time. She wasn't interested. She ignored the sudden warmth in her thigh…

Men did not interest her. Men in general did not figure large in her life, and with her father as an example it was hardly surprising. What with caring and worrying about her mother's health for most of her adult life—because her father certainly did not—she had never had the time for a boyfriend since she'd left school, even if she had wanted one. If her mother's doctor was right, she might soon have all the time in the world, and the knowledge made her want to weep. With sightless eyes she stared out of the window, a deep sigh escaping her.

Zac Delucca, for the first time in years, was stumped by a woman. The woman at his side was barely aware of his existence. Her uninterested responses to any attempt at conversation were mono-syllabic, and it irritated the hell out of him.

He had even resorted to allowing his thigh to brush against hers, and while it had done dangerous things to his libido she had dismissed the contact without a glance. He was definitely losing his touch, he thought, a wry grin twisting his firm lips.

'That was a big sigh. Is my company so boring?' He prompted sardonically.

The deep, dark tone of his voice reminded Sally where she was, and she turned her head to look at him. 'Not at all, Mr Delucca,' she replied coolly, and watched as he squared his impressively broad shoulders and casually stretched a long arm across the back of the seat behind her. Not touching, but somehow enclosing her. She drew in a shaky breath, not liking the unfamiliar weak sensation that he somehow aroused in her.

'Then please call me Zac,' he invited smoothly. Her face was a perfect social mask, but he had sensed her unease when he had moved closer. She was not as unaware of him as she appeared, and at last he had got her attention. 'I want there to be no formality between us, Sally,' he told her huskily.

In fact, he wanted nothing at all between them—not a stitch of clothing, just flesh on flesh. He had never felt so fiercely attracted to a woman in his life, and he watched her reaction as, unable to resist touching her, he allowed his long fingers to slide down and caress her shoulder.

She jumped like a scalded cat and shot back. 'I don't want anything at all between us.'

He could not prevent a chuckle as she verbalised his thought exactly, but he was pretty sure she was not thinking along the same lines as him.

'I'm glad you find me amusing,' she snapped, looking anything but amused. 'And take your hand off me.' She leant forward, shrugging her shoulder to dislodge his hand.

Zac let her, and settled back in the seat. Maybe he had made a mistake. Did he have the time to pursue her, and did he really want to? She was just another typical high-maintenance little rich girl, with her nose put out of joint because the doting father who kept her in comfort had refused to jump to her bidding.

The irony did not escape him. If Raffe's suspicions were correct, he had already paid for Sally Paxton's lifestyle without any of the benefits of keeping a beautiful woman.

He studied her for a long moment. She was incredibly lovely. Maybe he could make time. Her hands were folded in her lap, the soft swell of her breasts was just visible above the square-cut neckline of her dress, and her face was hauntingly beautiful but somehow sad. The end of an affair maybe… Easier for him if she was unattached…

'Not so amusing. More intriguing,' Zac finally responded, suddenly needing to know. 'Tell me— do you have a man in your life?'

Sally had heard the question countless times before. While she did not bother with men, quite a few bothered her, and she had developed a surefire way to cool their interest.

'No. Do you have a wife?' she retorted, glancing at him. He was still too close for her liking, his hard bicep touching her shoulder. Perhaps it wasn't deliberate—he was a big man, with an even bigger ego to match, she surmised, and put her plan into action. 'Because I never go out with married men.'

'No wife.' He smiled a hunter's smile, Sally thought. 'Nor do I want one,' he confirmed. Lifting one long finger, he swept a stray tendril of her hair around her ear and stroked down her cheek to tip her chin towards him. 'And no significant woman at the moment. So there isn't anything to prevent us getting together. I am a very generous lover, in bed and out. Trust me—I promise you will not be disappointed.'

The sheer arrogance of the man astounded Sally. She had only met him half an hour ago. Yet already he had told her he wasn't into commitment but was looking for an affair. Bottom line, she amended, he was looking for sex. Nothing more. Just like her dad.

She fought her instinctive reflex to knock his finger from her chin, and instead lifted wide blue eyes to his. They were dark and gleaming with masculine confidence. Well, not for long, she determined.

'Oh, I don't know, Zac,' she said huskily, and finally deliberately used his name. 'I am almost twenty-six, and I *do* want a husband—just not someone else's.' His finger fell from her chin. She caught the flicker of wariness in his dark eyes and wasn't surprised. Typical male reaction...

She gave him a wry smile. 'I too think it is good to be honest about one's intentions, as you so obviously are, Zac.' Sally doubted he noticed the underlying sarcasm in her tone. 'Therefore I feel I should do the same. Ideally, I would like to have three children, while I am young enough to enjoy them, so basically I do not have time to waste on an affair with you, even if I wanted to.'

The expression on his face was comical. From confident, ardent suitor to wary and outraged male in less than sixty seconds.

'I can assure you no woman has ever found an affair with me a waste of time,' he declared arrogantly, and she almost laughed out loud.

Unable to help herself, she expanded on the theme.

'If you say so.' She shrugged her shoulders. 'Then again, you must be—what? Thirty-six, seven...'

'Thirty-five,' he snapped.

He didn't like that, and Sally stifled a grin. 'Still, you're not getting any younger either. Maybe you will change your mind about marriage. You will certainly make someone a wonderful husband,' she complimented him, and was actually beginning to enjoy herself. He moved slightly, his arm no longer touching her shoulder, and for the first time since meeting him she actually gave him her whole attention.

She turned her back half against the window in order to face him, and deliberately let her big blue eyes roam slowly over him. His hair was silky black, with a tendency to curl, obviously controlled by superb styling. His eyes were heavy lidded, and at the moment narrowed, hiding his expression. His features were big: large nose, a wide mouth with perfectly chiselled lips, the bottom one slightly fuller, and a square jaw with a delightful indentation in his chin.

Actually, he was very attractive, Sally acknowledged. His shoulders were wide, his chest broad and his muscled thighs were stretching the fabric of his trousers, she noted as he moved further away and crossed the leg nearest to her over his other knee.

A student of body language would probably say that was a sign of rejection... Her ploy had worked, Sally thought. But to make sure, she added, 'You do have all the attributes to make a good husband—you're a fine figure of a man, fit and filthy rich.'

Zac had listened with growing disquiet as she spoke. The woman was after a husband—a rich husband. She was the same as all the rest of her species. Her saving grace, if one could call it that, was that at least she had put all her cards on the table up front.

Getting into anything with her would be a huge mistake, his inbuilt sense of survival screamed at him. But, when she had barely looked at him since they met, feeling her gorgeous blue eyes examining every inch of him had been the most erotic experience he had known in ages. Out of necessity he had crossed one leg over the other knee, to hide the wayward reaction of his body.

Thank the Lord the car was slowing down. In a minute they would be at the restaurant. A swift meal and a polite goodbye, and the fact he had trouble keeping his hands off this woman he would put down to his lengthy celibacy. His common sense was telling him this lady was dangerous to his peace of mind. Time to walk away.

He glanced at Sally. She was sitting back in the seat again, but her eyes were no longer cold. They were sparkling. He caught the glint of feline satisfaction in the blue depths, and her soft mouth quirked at the corners in a barely concealed grin.

The little devil! Had she been teasing him? Deliberately trying to put him off? He wasn't sure, and that was another first for him. Usually he could read a woman like a book, but this one had him tied in knots.

Warning bells rang loud and clear in his head, but he ignored them. He needed to delve a little deeper to discover what really made her tick. He had sensed her sadness and disappointment earlier—at her father or men in general he wasn't sure. She had done her best to ignore him, but then she had examined him with blatant female thoroughness and he knew she liked what she saw.

He was not a fool. He had felt her reaction the moment he had put a finger on her arm in the office, and again when he touched her cheek. She was not immune to him. But was she really looking for a wealthy husband?

Did he care? He had escaped that trap all his life, and he was smart enough to continue to do so. But he enjoyed a challenge, and Sally Paxton was definitely a challenge—one that he was determined to pursue and conquer.

She was an adult woman, not some shy young virgin, and he did not have to deprive his body of the pleasure of hers simply because she was looking for a husband, he concluded—to his own satisfaction.

CHAPTER THREE

THE restaurant was one of the best in London, and as they were led to their table by the *maître d'*, with Delucca's hand firmly in the small of her back, Sally began to wonder if she had been as clever as she thought at discouraging him.

Something had gone wrong. His hand was like a brand, burning through the raw silk of her dress, and if his reaction as he had helped her from the limousine was anything to go by she was in deep trouble. He had declared that now they knew where they stood they could get better acquainted over lunch.

He certainly didn't believe in wasting time, and she certainly did not want to get better acquainted with the man, she thought as her chair was held out for her and she sat down at the table. Briefly she looked around. There were more people leaving than arriving, and she glanced at the slim gold watch on her wrist. Not surprising, as it was two in the afternoon.

Suddenly, she was tired. She had been working all week, helping set up the latest exhibition to be staged at the museum. This morning the opening for the press and dignitaries had taken place, and she had attended at the request of her boss to answer any questions about the historical provenance of the exhibits. Usually she went to work in neat skirts and tops, but today she had dressed more smartly for the occasion. For months now she had been researching the history of the different exhibits, some of which had been brought up from the vast storage cellars and never been shown before.

Her boss knew of her mum's condition and had kindly allowed her to slip away at one o'clock. Almost two years of faithfully visiting her mother every weekend plus holidays, not to mention the constant worry, had taken their toll and she felt completely washed out.

The last thing she needed was to fight off the attentions of a predatory male. What she really needed was her bed…alone….

'Madam?'

She looked up. 'Sorry,' she murmured to the hovering *maître d'*, and took the menu.

'Perhaps you would prefer I order for you?'

There it was, that deep accented voice again, intruding on her thoughts. Reluctantly, Sally glanced across the table at her companion. For a moment their eyes met, and she recognised the challenging gleam in the depths of his before glancing down at the menu in her hand.

He was sitting there, all arrogant, powerful male, and she was about to refuse when she thought, why bother? The quicker he ordered, the quicker they ate, and the quicker she could get away from his disturbing presence. Because, being brutally honest, she recognised he *did* disturb her, in a way she had never felt before. But then he probably had the same effect on every woman on the planet. He was one hundred percent macho male, and then some…

No wonder he wasn't into commitment. Why would he settle for one woman when he had the pick of the best, according to the article she had read about him. It had extolled his brilliant business acumen and ended mentioning his preference for model girlfriends.

She certainly wasn't in his league, and nor did she want to be, she concluded firmly.

'Fine,' she said, and handed the menu back to the *maître d'*, and let her hand drop on the table, her fingers idly playing with a fork. She wasn't hungry—what did it matter what the man ordered?

'They do a very good steak here, and I can recommend the sea bass, but everything they serve is excellent.'

'The fish will be fine.'

'Fine,' Zac drawled with biting sarcasm. She was back to uninterested again. Grim-faced, he relayed the order to the *maître d'*, including a bottle of rather good wine. But inside he was seething.

Fine, she agreed when he mentioned the wine, without even looking at him. He had seen her glance at her watch as they arrived. He had never known any woman to be interested in the time when with him. Now she was sitting there, head bent, fiddling with a fork. Nobody ignored him— and certainly not a woman whose father had embezzled money out of a business of his. No matter how beautiful she was.

'Tell me, Sally, what do you do when you are not pressuring your father to take you to lunch?' he began silkily. 'Do you fill your days with shopping and visiting the beautician? Not that you need to…' He reached across and caught her hand in his, turning it over to examine the smooth palm. 'Does this soft hand actually do any work, or does Daddy keep you?'

Sally's head shot up as a tingling sensation snaked through her arm, and swiftly she pulled her hand free. Suddenly, she was intensely aware of Zac Delucca, in more ways than one. She was intelligent enough to know when she had been insulted. How typical of a super-rich tycoon like him to automatically think that simply because she had one Friday afternoon free her father supported her financially. Well, she was damned if she was going enlighten him. Let him keep his sexist attitude—she didn't care...

'I do shop—doesn't everyone?' she said nonchalantly. It was the truth. 'And I visit the hairdresser sometimes.' Again it was the truth. 'The rest of the time I read a lot.' Also the truth.

The food and wine arrived, interrupting the exchange, and Sally was grateful. She really wasn't up to sparring with the man any more. She had a feeling he was far too intelligent to be deceived by anything anyone said for long.

Zac filled her wine glass, although she had refused a drink. He insisted she try it. He offered her a piece of his steak on his fork, and she was so surprised by the intimacy of the gesture she actually took it.

He asked what her favourite film was. She said *Casablanca*, and he told her she was a hopeless romantic, then added that if he had been in Humphrey Bogart's position he would have taken the woman and run, which made her smile but somehow did not surprise her... His favourite film was *Cape Fear*, which she did find odd—until they got around to discussing books.

She told him she liked to read history and biographies, as well as being partial to the occasional murder story. And she discovered he spent most of his time reading financial journals and reports, but he did confess to reading the occasional thriller when he had time. Which figured, given *Cape Fear* was his first choice of film.

Sally sat back in her chair, replacing her knife and fork on the plate, surprised to note she had emptied her plate without realising. Against all expectations the lunch had been quite pleasant. Zac was a witty conversationalist, and he had made her smile—quite an accomplishment in her present state of mind.

She refused Zac's suggestion of a dessert and agreed to a coffee. He placed the order with the waiter, and Sally glanced around the restaurant again. The furnishings were elegant, the staff discreet, and it was obviously very expensive. Luckily, she was dressed for the occasion—not that she had expected to be here. The clientele were mostly wealthy, high-powered business people, she surmised. Of the few that were left she recognised a famous female presenter from the television and a well-known comedian.

'Sally Salmacis, as I live and breathe,' a voice called out.

Sally's eyes widened, and she pushed back her chair and leapt to her feet as six feet of shockingly ginger-haired male came striding towards her.

'Algernon!' she laughed.

Blue eyes met blue, and they grinned at each other, sharing a long-standing joke. Then she was swept up in a bear hug and kissed briefly on the lips, before being held at arm's length.

'Let me look at you. Gosh, you are more gorgeous than ever, Sally. How long has it been since I saw you? Two, three years?'

'About that,' she agreed. 'But what are you doing here?' she asked. 'I thought you were still collecting butterflies in the Amazon. I had visions of you being eaten alive by mosquitoes.'

'Yes, well, not quite—but not far off. You know me. I never could stand the heat.'

'Hardly surprising.' She arched one delicate eyebrow. 'I did warn you, Al.' His complexion, if anything, was even fairer than hers.

They had met at primary school, two redheads with unusual names, and had naturally gravitated towards each other as protection against the bullies. Al was the only person who dared to use her given name. She had demanded even her parents must call her Sally after her first year at school, and Algernon had done the same, demanding his parents call him Al. As teenagers they had planned on taking a year off after university to go around the world together, starting with South America— Al for the butterflies, and Sally to see the ruins of Machu Picchu. Her mum's illness had put an end to Sally's dream, but she still lived with the faint hope that she would do it one day.

'So what are you up to?' she queried, delighted to see him again.

'Working in the family firm with Dad. We had just finished lunch, and I was following him out when I spotted you. But what about you? Still studying the Ancients?' he prompted with a grin.

'Yes.' She grinned back.

'I have to dash, but give me your new number. I tried your old with no joy.' He took his cell phone out of his pocket and entered the number as Sally told him.

Zac Delucca had seen and heard enough. The telephone number was the final straw. For a woman with no man in her life, this guy, if not now, obviously had been. He had never seen Sally so animated—certainly not with him. When he had heard the younger man speak to her, then seen him take her in his arms and kiss her, he had been blinded by a red tide of sheer male jealousy—not an emotion he was familiar with, and it had stunned him for a moment. But not any more…

'Sally, darling.' He rose to his feet and crossed to her side. 'You must introduce me to your friend,' he demanded, fixing the young man with a gimlet-eyed stare.

Suddenly remembering where she was and who

she was with, Sally swiftly made the introduction. She saw Al flinch as Zac shook his hand. The man was demonstrating his superior strength like a rutting bull, she though disgustedly. And where did he get off, calling her darling?

Al, ever the gentleman, responded politely. 'Pleased to meet you Mr Delucca. A shame our meeting has to be so brief.' He gave Sally an apologetic glance. 'Sorry, Sally, I can't stay and talk. You know Dad, he will be waiting outside. champing at the bit to get back to work. I'm going to a house party this weekend, but I will call you next week and we can have dinner and catch up. What do you say?'

It took a brave man to stand up to Delucca, but Al refused to be intimidated and Sally gave her old friend a gentle smile.

'Yes, that would be lovely,' she said, and watched him walk out.

She resumed her seat as the waiter arrived with their coffee, her eyes misty with memories of a happier time. Al had never teased her about the stutter she had developed as a child after the death of her grandmother, who had lived with them. He had been her staunch defender and best friend all through her school years. He had attended every birthday party she had, and been a frequent visitor to her home. And she had spent countless summer days playing around the swimming pool at his home, a magnificent thirties-style Art Deco house situated in Sandbanks, overlooking Poole Harbour.

He had been the first boy to kiss her, and he had been as shy as her. The sex side of things had not progressed much further than a few tentative gropes which had made them giggle, and they'd realised they were more brother and sister than lovers.

They had drifted apart since leaving school. She had gone to university in Exeter, while Al had gone to Oxford to study botany, much against his father's wishes. They had kept in touch, and met up in the holidays occasionally, but with her mum's illness, gradually their only contact had become the occasional telephone call or chance meeting, like today.

The last time she had seen him had been when they had bumped into each other in Bournemouth and gone for a drink. Al had been all fired up with the Amazon trip he was about to embark on, and had asked Sally to go with him. She had reluctantly refused, explaining that her mum was in the clear, but that she, Sally, was about to start a great new job in London.

It seemed a lifetime ago now…

'Very touching.' A deep, mocking voice cut into her memories. 'Al is an old friend, I take it? Or should I say lover?'

She looked across at Zac, caught the latent anger in his eyes, and realised that beneath the cool, sophisticated exterior he was not pleased. Well, she was not a happy bunny either. She had not wanted to go to lunch with the man in the first place.

'Say what you like. It is no business of yours.'

'It is my business. When I take a lady out to lunch I expect her to behave like a lady, not leap up into another man's arms—a man who yells her name, *Sally!*—and when he demands "*Sal my kiss*" proceeds to kiss him.'

Sally was puzzled for a moment, then her blue eyes widened in understanding. Her lips twitched and, unable to help herself, she burst out laughing. Of all the nicknames she had been called at school—*salami*, or simply *sausage* being the favourites—no one had ever put *that* interpretation on her birth name.

'I'm glad you found it amusing because I didn't.' His accent had thickened and the anger in the black eyes that blazed into hers was all too real.

If that was what he had thought, in a way she could see his point, and she decided to tell him the truth.

'You were mistaken. Al did not ask me for a kiss.' She grinned. 'My first name is not Sally but Salmacis.' She gave him the proper pronunciation, a syllable at a time. '*Sal-ma-sis.*' And saw disbelief, puzzlement and finally curiosity in his dark eyes.

Zac didn't know whether to believe her. Salmacis was not a name he had ever heard in any language, and he knew half a dozen. If it was an excuse it was a hell of a good one. Yet she looked sincere, and English was not his first language, he could have been mistaken.

'Salmacis.' He rolled the name off his tongue and rather liked it. 'What kind of name is that?'

'It is Greek. When my mum was pregnant with me she spent the last four months of her pregnancy on bedrest. She got hooked on reading Greek mythology.'

Then Sally told him the legend. 'Apparently Salmacis was the nymph of a fountain near Halicarnassus in Asia Minor. She became one with the youth Hermaphroditos. And before you ask, no, I am not a hermaphrodite—but I believe that is the origin of the word.'

'It never entered my head.' Zac chuckled. 'What possessed your mother to give you such a peculiar though rather lovely name?' he demanded, still smiling broadly. 'You have to admit it is extremely unusual.'

For a moment Sally was stunned, her heart racing out of control as she met his enquiring gaze. His dark eyes danced with golden lights, his hard face was transformed into a softer, younger version by the brilliance of his smile, and she could not help smiling back at him.

'I think it was the last fable she read before

going into labour, and unfortunately for me it stuck in her mind,' she said wryly.

'No, not unfortunate. You are far too exotic—no, that isn't the word.' Zac shook his dark head, searching his brain for the English equivalent of what he wanted to say. 'Your beauty is too unique. No—too mystical for a Sally,' he declared with satisfaction. 'Salmacis suits you much better.' He saw the humour in her expressive eyes. How had he ever thought they were cold?

'I much prefer Sally—in fact, I insist on it. So be warned— call me Salmacis and I will ignore you.'

'Okay—Sally,' he conceded, and added, 'But I am a little surprised she persuaded your father to agree to such an unusual name. Accountants are not known for their flights of fancy.'

The sparkle vanished from her eyes like a light being switched off, to be replaced with a familiar blank look.

'She didn't have to. My dad married Mum because he got her pregnant when she was eighteen and he was thirty-five,' Sally told Zac. It was the truth. Exhaustion from her hectic work schedule and from worrying about her mother overtook her, and she could not be bothered to dissemble.

'Apparently, he was so upset when the doctor told him she would not have any more children, no future son, he didn't much care what name I was given.'

Appalled by Sally's matter-of-fact revelation, Zac realised her father's attitude must have hurt her. To actually let the child know how he'd felt was a disgraceful thing to do. But then Nigel Paxton was almost certainly a thief and an unfaithful husband: sensitivity was obviously not his strong point.

'I think we should leave now.' Her voice intruded on his thoughts. 'We are the only couple left.'

Zac had not noticed, but glancing around the room he saw she was right.

When was the last time a woman had held his attention to the exclusion of everything else around him? he asked himself. Never. The realisation shocked him rigid. In that moment he determined there was no way he was going to let it happen again. Sally was as dangerous as she was beautiful, and she was not for him...

'Finish your coffee and we will go,' he agreed, and beckoned the *maître d'*. He handed him a credit card and a bundle of notes for a tip, and after draining his coffee cup stood up.

The meal had turned out okay, despite its difficult start, and he had learnt a lot about Salmacis—too much, he thought wryly. From what he had overheard earlier, Sally obviously knew about her father's infidelity and resented the fact he had more time for a girlfriend than he had for her. Hence turning up at the office today and demanding her father lunch with her.

Money obviously was not enough for the lovely Salmacis; she was the type who craved attention from the men in her life. Given the reaction of her father to her name, he could understand why she behaved the way she did. But clinging, needy women did not appeal to him, he rationalised, confirming his decision not to see her again.

He glanced down at her. She looked fragile and, act or not, he couldn't prevent himself from slipping an arm around her waist as he led her out of the restaurant. She made no attempt to pull away, another first, but leant against him as they walked to where the limo was parked a few yards away.

He let the chauffeur help her inside.

She was magic to hold, he thought ruefully as he slipped into the back seat beside her, but every male instinct he possessed told him this was one woman he was going to pass on—for his own preservation.

'Where would you like us to drop you off?' he asked. 'Bond Street? Harrods?' he suggested, with an edge of cynicism in his tone.

'Harrods is fine.'

He'd thought as much. A bit of retail therapy was all any woman needed to keep her happy.

She looked up at him with soft blue eyes, and he could not resist. He wrapped an arm around her

waist and slid his hand through the silken tumble
of her hair to tip up her face.

'What are you doing?' she murmured.

'Oh, I think you know,' he drawled huskily, and
covered her lush lips with his own.

He could not let her go without kissing and
tasting her just once, he told himself...

CHAPTER FOUR

STARTLED out of her lethargy as a strong arm slipped around her waist, Sally arched back in instinctive denial of the intimacy he was seeking. She glanced up at his darkly attractive face and recognised the sensual intent in his eyes. She was stunned by the sudden flash of awareness that heated her whole body. He was going to kiss her...

Her pulse began to race, and as his dark head bent she could almost feel the virile power emanating from his mighty frame. For a second she was tempted to abandon herself to what he was offering. But she knew it would be a disastrous mistake. She had no time in her life for an affair with Zac or any other man, even if she wanted one. She put her hands up to push him away, but too late...

Zac's warm mouth claimed hers with a soft sensuality that totally confused and captivated her. She closed her eyes, her lips involuntarily parting to accept the subtle intrusion of his tongue as he deepened the kiss with a skilful, seductive passion that blew all thought of resistance from her mind.

Sally had never experienced a kiss like it. Dizzy with a sensual excitement she had never known before, she let her mouth cling to his, and eagerly, if a little inexpertly, returned the passion. Suddenly he broke the kiss, and tiny moans of regret escaped her, quickly followed by a gasp of pleasure as he trailed kisses down her throat and lower, to trace with his tongue the gentle curve of her breasts revealed by the neckline of her dress.

His hand dropped to slip beneath the fabric, long fingers edging beneath the delicate lace of her bra to cup her naked breast, a thumb teasing the burgeoning tip to send rivers of unbelievable sensation flowing through her body. His mouth returned to hers, and she was enthralled by his taste, his touch, drowning in the sea of erotic pleasure his kisses and caresses evoked. She felt the heat of his palm on her bare leg, his hand stroking up her thigh, and she trembled, the blood pulsing thick and fast through her veins. She was ablaze with sensuous hunger, with a need she didn't understand but knew she wanted fulfilled badly.

So this was what she had been missing—this was the reason people loved sex, she thought wonderingly, and curved her hand around his neck to mesh her fingers in the silken hair of his head.

Abruptly he pulled away, and without his support Sally flopped back against the seat. Lost in a haze of sexual arousal, she murmured, 'What happened?'

'We have arrived at your destination. Harrods.'

His deep accented voice speared like an icicle through the emotional fog clouding her brain. She was mortified. She had not noticed the car had stopped. She glanced down and, horrified, adjusted the bodice of her dress. She looked out of the window—anywhere but at the man next to her. Finally, as the silence lengthened, reluctantly she looked back at Zac Delucca.

He was watching her, his eyes as dark as night, the remnants of desire swirling in the liquid depths.

'Shame, I know, Sally.' His lips quirked at the corners in the beginnings of a smile. 'But we can continue this later. Have dinner with me tonight.'

'No,' she said abruptly. Sally had never felt so embarrassed and ashamed in her life. Noting her skirt had hitched up around her thighs, she swiftly smoothed it down with trembling hands. Never in all her life had a man kissed and touched her so intimately. And she couldn't understand what had come over her.

'Tomorrow night, then,' he prompted.

How the hell had it happened? Sally asked herself for the second time today in the luxury of his limousine. This time it was much worse, and it was Zac Delucca's fault again. When he had spoken of his skills as a lover she had never dreamt he meant to try and prove his statement with such explicit speed that the defensive wall she had built around herself would crumble with just one kiss…

'Sorry, no. I am going away for the weekend.'

'Cancel and spent the weekend with me,' he demanded arrogantly.

Staring at him, her blue eyes widening, Sally unconsciously ran the tip of her tongue over her slightly swollen lips, where the taste of Zac still lingered. It would be so easy to say yes to a weekend of mindless pleasure instead of sadness, and suddenly she was afraid of the speed with which he had turned her life upside down. Then she realised he had been nowhere near as affected by the passionate interlude as she had been, and, given the churning in her stomach, still was!

He probably seduced women in his limo on a regular basis, and she had very nearly been his latest conquest…

She thought of her mother, who really needed her, as opposed to a man like Delucca, who certainly did not—except in the shallowest way. Zac was undoubtedly a formidable man, used to getting whatever and whoever he wanted, and he was her father's new boss.

But then again, Sally thought, she didn't give a fig for her father. If she offended his boss, so what?

'That's an outrageous suggestion and not one I would ever consider,' she said bluntly. 'And I promised my mother.'

'Loyalty to your mother is an admirable trait. We can make it dinner on Monday night.'

Not only was he arrogant, he was also pig-headed, and she did not bother to reply as, to her relief, the chauffeur opened the car door. She needed to get as far away from Zac Delucca as she could, and, swinging her legs out of the car, she stood up. She hesitated and glanced back at Zac. Good manners were ingrained in her.

'Thank you for lunch, Mr Delucca, and the lift,' she said formally. 'Goodbye.' And, turning, she hurried along the street.

She did not go into the store, Zac noted as he watched her walk along the pavement. Her rear view was as enticing as the rest of her, and the reason he had eschewed good manners and not helped her out of the limousine was still causing him a problem.

'Drive on,' he ordered the chauffeur. Sally—or Salmacis, he smiled to himself—intrigued and also confused him.

By nature he was a decisive man. Once he decided on a course of action in both the business world and his private life he never changed his mind. Yet a certain red-haired woman had him changing his mind over and over again.

Needy was a no-no; husband-hunting was a no-no; idle little rich girl was a no-no—and he did not believe for a minute that she was spending the weekend with her mother. Partying was more her style, if the slight violet shadows under her beautiful eyes were anything to go by. He would bet on it… She wasn't his usual type at all.

Yet, against all that, after deciding to kiss her goodbye he had changed his mind again.

As soon as their lips had met she had caught fire in his arms, melting against him, running her fingers through his hair, inflaming him further. She was the most incredibly responsive woman he had ever met, and there was no way he was walking away.

He strolled back into Paxton's office and glanced at Raffe, who shook his head slightly. So Paxton did not know yet they were on to him. Good.

'Your daughter and I had a pleasant lunch, Paxton. She asked to be dropped off at Harrods, though I noticed she didn't go in the store.'

'You know what young women are like—always changing their minds,' he said with an ingratiating smile. 'I gave her a studio apartment in Kensington and it is not far from Harrods. She probably decided to walk home.'

Zac knew enough about property in London to know that an apartment in the Royal Borough of Kensington did not come cheap. Sally was a lucky girl, and Paxton was looking guiltier by the minute.

Sally drove into the car park of the nursing home and cut the engine. She glanced up at the mellow stone, half covered by the rampant scarlet Virginia creeper. The sun was shinning, it was a glorious June day, and yet she felt none of the joy such a beautiful day should bring. For a moment she folded her arms across the steering wheel and let her head drop. She had to smile for her mother, even though her heart felt like lead in her chest. It was hard…so very hard… Even more so now she knew the doctor's prognosis…

As she had guessed, her father had not rung her last night, and she had had no luck in getting in touch with him until this morning, when he'd informed her that because Delucca was there he could not possibly get away this weekend.

For once Sally believed him. After yesterday's lunch with the man, she knew no one could refuse him—herself included. She still cringed when she thought of the way she had reacted to his kiss and, worse, the way she had spent a restless night trying to banish him from her mind—without much success.

Lifting her head, she drew in a deep, steadying breath and brushed a stray drop of moisture from her eye. At least today she would not have to lie to her mother. Her dad *was* tied up with business.

Five minutes later, forcing a smile to her face, Sally breezed into her mother's room with a cheerful hello.

She was sitting in her wheelchair, an expectant smile on her face—a still lovely face, although now it was deeply lined with pain. Her hair was no longer the soft red Sally remembered. After her chemo it had grown back a mousy brown, and was now streaked with grey.

Yet her mum had not given up, Sally thought as she walked towards her. She had still applied her make-up—and even if the foundation was a bit streaky and the lipstick not perfect she had tried… Probably because she expected her husband. But she was destined to be disappointed yet again.

Sally swallowed the lump that formed in her throat, and dropped a soft kiss on her lined cheek.

The nurse had dressed her mum in the pretty summer frock Sally had bought for her the week before. She always brought a gift when she visited—sometimes simply a box of chocolates. This week she had book on Greek Mythology she had found in a secondhand bookstore. It was a real find as it was a very old copy, printed in 1850, with wonderful illustrations.

She gave her mum the book, and she was delighted, but her smile faded a little when Sally told her her husband was not coming. Sally tried to make it better by explaining about his new boss, saying that she had actually met him at her dad's office, and that seemed to satisfy her.

Later Sally suggested they take a walk in the garden as it was such a perfect afternoon. Her mum agreed, and she spent a pleasant hour pushing the wheelchair around the extensive grounds.

Sally sighed as she entered the studio apartment gifted to her by her parents and closed the door behind her. She sagged against it. It had been another beautiful summer day, but she felt hot, sticky and tired.

The weekend had been bittersweet. She had not left her mum until late last night. The outing in the garden had tired her, and Sally had helped the nurse put her to bed and then sat with her for the rest of the afternoon and Saturday evening. She had done the same on Sunday, and it had been after midnight when she'd finally arrived back in London, exhausted. But worry over her mother and the images of a tall dark man had fractured her sleep, and she had had to drag herself out of bed this morning to go to work.

She felt totally worn out, both mentally and physically, and for a moment hadn't the strength to move. Shoulders slumped, she glanced around the room with jaundiced eyes. She hated the place.

It had been her father's studio apartment for years, but after her mum's accident he had sold the family home in Bournemouth and bought a three-bedroomed apartment in fashionable Notting Hill.

How he had persuaded her mother to sell the house in Bournemouth—the house her mum had inherited from her parents—Sally had had no idea, but she had reluctantly agreed to go and see the new apartment, supposedly the new family home. It was a top-floor conversion of a large Georgian house, and she'd swiftly realised it was unsuitable for a wheelchair—which to her mind simply confirmed that her father had no intention of ever living with his wife again.

His excuse for selling the house was the cost of keeping his wife in the nursing home. As it was he who had put her there, it did not cut much ice with Sally, but she could not deny he did pay the fees.

Then, to her dismay, she had found herself the recipient of his studio apartment. Her mother had been delighted, and told her it was time she had a place of her own. When she'd tried to refuse her mother had insisted, and told her to listen to her father—he was the accountant, and the property was a good investment. Apparently, giving the studio to Sally was a great way of avoiding death duties in the future!

Sally had then realised how he had persuaded her mum to sell, and it had confirmed in her mind what a greedy low-life he really was...

She had reluctantly moved in ten months ago, when the lease on her old apartment ran out, mainly because her mother had kept asking her when she was going to move.

But to Sally this apartment didn't feel like her home, and she knew it never could—because in her head she would always think of it as her dad's sleazy love-nest. A fact that had been brought home to her the first week she'd moved in, when she'd fielded quite a few calls from present and previously discarded mistresses. She had changed the telephone number, but she could not change the fact that a string of women other than his wife had shared the king-size bed.

As a studio apartment it was a superior example, with natural wooden floors, and it was larger than most. The kitchen and bathroom were off the small entrance hall, separate from the main living area which was split-level, with a mini-staircase leading to the bedroom area. She had thrown out every piece of furniture her father had left, including his king-size bed and the mirror over it, and bought a queen-size bed for herself.

She had redecorated completely, in neutral tones, and bought the minimum of new furniture: a sofa, an occasional table, and a television for the living area. In the bedroom she had fitted interlocking beechwood units along one wall, which included drawers and shelves where she could house her books, plus a desktop that stretched the length of one unit. It held her computer and doubled as a dressing table. The other wall had a built-in wardrobe with mirrored doors. The bed had a beechwood head-board, and all her bedlinen was plain white—easily interchangeable. She didn't need anything else, and she probably would not be there much longer.

She had mentioned to her mother a month ago that she was thinking of trying to sell the studio, telling her she would really prefer a separate bedroom. Her mum had said that would be nice, and the subject had not been mentioned again. But Sally had placed it with a local estate agent the next Monday. She had stipulated that she wanted no sign outside, as she was at work all day and away every weekend and a sign tended to encourage burglars.

She need not have bothered, as she no longer cared whether she sold it or not. Since hearing the doctor's prognosis for her mother last week she'd recognised there were a lot worse things in life than living in an apartment one didn't like.

She straightened up and headed for the kitchen, dropping her purse on the sofa on the way. A cup of coffee, a sandwich and a shower, in that order, and then bed.

Checking the water level in the kettle, she switched it on, and, opening a cupboard, reached for a jar of instant coffee just as the wall-mounted telephone rang.

Her heart leapt in panic. It must be the nursing home about her mother, was her first thought, and, lifting the receiver from the rest, she said quickly, 'Sally here—what is it?'

'Not what—who,' a deep voice corrected her with a chuckle, before continuing, unnecessarily identifying himself. 'Zac.' And she nearly dropped the phone.

'How did you get my number?' she demanded.

'Easy. Your father told me you lived in Kensington. I wasn't so obvious as to ask him for your number, but you *are* in the telephone book.'

Of course she was. Hadn't she changed the number and registered it under her own name? 'You looked through all the Paxtons in the book? You must have had to ring dozens to find me.' She couldn't believe a man of his wealth and stature would go to so much trouble.

'No. Surprisingly there are only a few, and yours was the first number I tried. I am just naturally lucky, Sally.'

He was naturally arrogant as well—and what was she doing, bothering to talk to him?

'Now, about tonight,' he continued. 'I've booked a table for eight.' He mentioned a famous Mayfair restaurant.

'Wait a damn minute,' Sally cut in angrily. 'I never agreed to go out to dinner with you. So thanks, but no thanks, I am staying in to wash my hair,' she ended sarcastically, and hung up.

Her heart pounded in her chest, and she pulled in some deep breaths to control the anger and—if she was honest—the excitement the sound of his deep-toned voice aroused so easily.

The kettle boiled, and she made a cup of coffee with a hand that was not quite steady. What was happening to her? Exhaustion—that was the problem. It had probably lowered her immune system and sent her emotions haywire. Satisfied with the explanation, she made a cheese sandwich with stale bread, but ate most of it anyway and drank her coffee.

She crossed to the bed area, slipping out of her skirt, and she hung it in the closet and headed for the bathroom. She stripped naked, and, dropping her blouse, bra and briefs into the wash basket, turned the shower on to warm. She picked up a bottle of shampoo from the vanity unit and stepped under the soothing spray.

She washed her hair and then, placing the shampoo on the chrome rack, she let her head fall back. She closed her eyes and let the water wash away the grime and hopefully the grimness of the weekend.

Her mother had been pleased to see her, and had declared she was perfectly content, but Sally knew different. No matter how good the nursing home, how great the staff were or how beautiful the gardens, it was still a nursing home. The patients were there out of necessity, because they needed constant care. She doubted anyone, given a choice, would choose it over their own home.

She shrugged off her morbid thoughts, and, switching off the shower, grabbed a large fluffy towel from the towel rail and rubbed her body dry. She towel-dried her hair, deciding not to bother with the hairdryer, and letting it hang down her back to dry naturally. She cleaned her teeth at the basin, and, taking her towelling robe off the hook on the back of the bathroom door, she slipped it on, tying the sash firmly around her waist.

The telephone rang as she walked back into the living room. Surely not Delucca again? Moving to the kitchen, she answered it with a curt, 'Yes?'

'My. Sally, who has rattled your cage?' an old familiar voice demanded.

'Al!' She laughed. 'I thought it was someone else.'

'Not the guy you were having lunch with, I hope?'

'Got it in one.'

'Sally, be careful. I mentioned I had met Delucca to my dad. According to him the man is not the type to get involved with. Apparently, he is an extremely powerful man, admired by a few, but feared by most. He is known as the takeover king and he's a brilliantly astute businessman. Delucca Holdings is one of the few companies that the recession has barely affected—mainly because he is ruthless at closing down failing companies and selling off their assets. But he's equally as clever at retaining and expanding the profitable ones. He owns mines in South America and Australia, a couple of oil companies, land and a lot more besides. As my dad pointed out, all tangible assets that, unlike stocks and shares, in the long term can't fail. As for his private life, not much is known about him except that he has dated quite a few top models.'

'I know all that—and don't worry. I refused his offer of dinner. The lunch was a one-off, never to be repeated.'

'Great. So have dinner with *me* tomorrow night? I have a table booked for nine at the new *in* place, but the girl I had high hopes of turned me down.'

'That is a back-handed invite if ever I heard one.' She laughed, but agreed, and after ten minutes of talking to Al she felt revived and almost human again.

She switched on the television, and an hour later was curled up on the sofa, watching the ending of her favourite crime programme and contemplating going to bed, when the doorbell rang.

The building had a concierge, and the intercom had not rung to announce anyone's arrival, so it had to be Miss Telford from across the hall, Sally guessed. She had met her the first week she had moved in, when the elderly spinster had locked herself out. Since then, at Miss Telford's request, Sally had kept a spare set of keys for her apartment, just in case she did it again—which she did quite frequently...

Standing up and stretching, Sally switched off the television and padded barefoot across the floor to open the door.

'Forgotten the key...? You!' The surprised exclamation left her lips before she could prevent it.

Sally was struck dumb, her incredulous gaze sweeping over the man before her. Zac Delucca was standing in the doorway, with what looked like a large cooler box in one hand and a bunch of roses in the other.

'An honest woman—you actually were washing your hair,' he drawled, eyeing the damp tousled curls falling around her shoulders. 'But washing your hair or not, Sally, I figured you still need to eat. These are for you.' He held out the roses and she took them, too shocked to refuse, and then, brushing past her, he strolled into her apartment. 'Nice place,' he opined, and set the box on the occasional table before turning round to look at her.

Still speechless, Sally let her eyes roam in helpless admiration over his impressive form. Gone was the designer suit. In its place he was wearing a white cotton shirt, and denim jeans that hung low on his lean hips and faithfully moulded his strong thighs and long legs. The designer label was a discreet signature on a side pocket.

Involuntarily her gaze was drawn back to his broad muscular chest, outlined by the obviously tailor-made shirt, the first few buttons of which were unfastened, revealing the strong column of his throat and a tantalising glimpse of black chest hair. Sally gulped, and for a moment had an overwhelming urge to run her fingers through the curling body hair. She took a step forward, the basic animal magnetism of the man, drawing her like a moth to a flame…

But the door slamming shut behind her brought her to her senses, and she ruthlessly squashed the impulse and found her voice.

'The doorman never called, so how the hell did

you get in?' she demanded, and lifted her eyes to his face; now he was grinning broadly, and looked even more devastatingly attractive, Sally thought helplessly.

'I told him you were my lover and it was our one month anniversary. I said I wanted to surprise you with champagne and roses and an intimate dinner for two. The man is clearly a romantic at heart—he could not refuse. Plus the tip helped,' he added cynically.

There it was again. No one ever refused Zac Delucca. And Sally had a sinking sensation that if she was not very careful she might fall into that category too.

She went on the attack. 'Then the man is going to lose his job, because I did not invite you here. I want you to leave now—get out or I will throw you out…' She raised angry blue eyes to his and caught a golden flame of desire in the dark depths so fierce she imagined she felt the heat—before his attention was diverted from her face…

CHAPTER FIVE

LOOKING at Zac, towering over her Sally had the wild desire to laugh at her own audacity in threatening to eject him. But as the silence lengthened a desire of a different kind whipped any thought of laughter from her mind. She saw he was scrutinising her slender body with an intensity that made her feel as if he was stripping her naked.

Suddenly, tension thickened the air between them, and it became hard for Sally to breathe. She felt a ripple of heat run through her, and it had nothing to do with the heat of the day.

Zac seemed to fill the small studio with his presence, and however unwillingly she was being drawn towards him despite all her best efforts to deny the fact. His dark eyes lingered on the open lapels of her robe, and jerkily she pulled the belt tighter, remembering she actually was naked underneath...

Embarrassment and the hot flush of arousal combined to make a tide of pink stain her pale face.

He stared at her for a long moment, and she wished she had done something with her hair instead of leaving it to dry in a mess of curls—ridiculous, she knew, but he had that effect on her.

'You would not cost the man his job. I know you are not that mean-spirited, Sally,' he said with certainty. He was right, damn him. 'As for throwing me out—you haven't a chance. But you are welcome to try.' And he walked towards her, throwing his arms wide. 'This should be interesting,' he prompted and grinned at her. Her heart missed a beat at the devilish charm of his expression. 'Give it your best shot.'

He was looming over her like some great monolith, legs slightly splayed, arms outstretched. She knew he was laughing at her, but still she had an incredible urge to walk into his arms.

'Very funny,' she snapped, and looked away. She knew when she was beaten. But as she stepped to one side an imp of mischief made her smack his forearm with the bunch of roses she still held in her hand. As a tension reliever it worked…

'That hurt!' she heard him yelp, and this time she did laugh as she dashed to the kitchen to put the somewhat battered roses in water.

She took a vase from the cupboard where she kept her glasswear, and, filling it with water, put the roses in one at a time. They were magnificent blooms—or had been, she amended, before they had met the strength of Zac's arm. And suddenly she felt a little guilty as she placed the vase on the windowsill.

'Truce?' He came up behind her, and she turned. He was too close, his big body crowding her. She caught the elusive scent of his aftershave—or was it simply him?—and her pulse began to race. She had difficulty holding his gaze.

'You have already drawn my blood.' He held up his arm.

Sally looked down, and to her horror realised she had. His bronzed, hair-dusted forearm bore a small scratch, and she saw the thin line of blood and felt even guiltier. 'I'm so sorry—let me put a plaster—'

'Not necessary.' He cut her off. 'But in recompense the least you can do is let me feed you.'

Warily, she looked up into his darkly attractive face. She didn't trust him, and worse she did not trust herself around him.

'I do mean only to feed you.'

He seemed to possess the ability to read her mind. 'Okay,' she finally said—mainly because she was thoroughly ashamed of herself. She wasn't by nature a violent person, but Zac Delucca brought out a host of violent sensations in her she had never realised she possessed. And, given that she had ripped his arm open with the roses he had bought her, it seemed the least she could do…

'Good.' And, reaching into the cupboard she had left open, he withdrew two glasses. 'I will deal with the wine and let you get the cutlery we need. Everything else is provided.'

'Fine. Do you want to eat here?' she asked, glancing at the fold-down table and two stools against one wall of the kitchen, where she usually ate, and then back to Zac. She grimaced. If he stretched his arms out again he could reach from wall to wall.

'It is a bit cramped, but it is either here or the living room.'

'The living room,' he decided, and, swinging on his heels, walked out of the kitchen.

Sally opened a drawer and withdrew knives, forks and spoons, wondering what she had let herself in for. She had let her guilt at lashing out at Zac override her common sense and agreed to him staying. Now she was not so sure. He disturbed her on so many levels. He had barged his way into her home uninvited, and yet the memory of the steamy kiss they had shared in the car still lingered. And if she was honest she would not mind repeating the experience. Anyway, what harm could it do to share a meal with him?

An hour later, licking her lips after finishing off dessert—a perfect Tiramisu—Sally was confident there had been no harm at all…

Actually, it had been a great meal. When she'd exited the kitchen with the plates and cutlery, Zac had already filled the occasional table with an assortment of dishes: delicious pasta, fresh crusty bread and Veal Milanese, as well as salad and the dessert.

He had got the food from his favourite Italian restaurant, owned by a friend of his, he'd told her, and had made her laugh with stories of the proprietor and his family. Then he'd opened a bottle of wine and filled her glass and his, and made a toast to friendship.

Zac had been charming—a perfect gentleman. He had taken care not to so much as touch her, and there was still a foot of space between them on the sofa. Nothing like the arrogant man she had met last Friday, who had hardly kept his hands off her.

In fact, apart from Al, she could not remember ever feeling so relaxed in a man's company. But then maybe seeing her with no make-up, wet hair and wearing a tired old robe had dampened Zac's ardour, she thought with a wry grin, and told herself she was glad. But a little voice in her head whispered that it would be nice to feel his arms around her once more...

'That was wonderful,' she said, casting a sidelong glance at Zac. He was lounging back on the sofa beside her, his long legs stretched out before him, a glass of wine in his hand. His big body was at ease, and she had the fanciful notion that he looked like some great half-slumbering jungle predator.

'An apple and a stale cheese sandwich are no substitute for a good meal,' she went on, telling herself she was being ridiculous, fantasising about Zac. Picking up her glass of wine, she drained it and replaced it on the table. She raised a hand to her mouth as a yawn overtook her. Too much wine and not enough sleep, she thought, and murmured a polite, 'Thank you.'

'My pleasure,' he drawled, turning towards her, a smile curving his hard mouth. His dark eyes met hers and she smiled lazily back, feeling strangely comfortable with Zac. Then his gaze dropped to where the soft blue fabric of her robe hugged the firm mounds of her breasts, unexpectedly making her shiver with sensual awareness.

Sally flushed and looked away. Suddenly, from being relaxed and sleepy she was wide-awake, and the sexual tension that had simmered between them when he arrived was back in full force. Her heart thudded a little faster and she had to swallow hard before she could find her voice.

'Now I think you'd better leave. I am rather tired,' she said defensively, shocked at how quickly he could arouse her with just a look.

'So thank me properly and I will,' Zac prompted softly, placing his glass on the table. He studied her pale beautiful face. Sally had actually yawned—not the effect he usually had on women. Though he noted the violet shadows under her eyes had deepened. Too much fun over the weekend...

Yet this exquisite creature had been driving him mad all evening. He had tried looking across the room, but the convenience of the bed, with its pristine white covers, had simply increased his frustration. He had thought she looked gorgeous elegantly dressed. But now, lounging on the sofa, with no make-up and wearing only a long blue bathrobe that exactly matched her eyes, with the silken mass of her glorious hair falling around her shoulders, she looked sensational.

After the first glass of wine she had unbent a little, and by the second she'd started eating and obviously enjoying the food. But had she been aware that every time she'd reached for a dish the lapels of her robe had gaped open, revealing her perfect breasts down to the dusky pink areolae? Or that when she licked her full lips she almost gave him a coronary? By accident or design he was not sure, and that yawn could have been fake... He didn't care. His patience was running out.

'A freely given kiss will be enough,' he prompted huskily, and raised his hand to the side of her elegant neck, felt the pulse beating furiously in her throat, and was encouraged to let his fingers slide through the heavy fall of her silken curls—something he had been itching to do since she answered the door to him, looking gorgeous, with damp tousled hair and ready for bed...

'Fine—as long as you realise that is all it will be, Zac.' Her voice was soft, and she met his dark eyes cautiously.

'Of course. I would not do anything you did not want me to,' he assured her, and hoped this time it would be *fine*. He had noticed she had the habit of using the word when the opposite was true.

Edging closer, her slender thigh touching his, she moved to press her soft lips against his cheek.

'You call that a kiss?' He growled his frustration just as she was about to draw back, and placing one hand behind her head, looped the other arm around her waist and tugged her against him. She gave him a startled glance and tried to shake her head, but he held her firm and kissed her with all the pent-up passion that had been riding him ever since he had set eyes on her.

She responded as he had known she would, her arms reaching up to clasp his shoulders. He deepened the kiss, the taste, the heat, the scent of her enflaming all his senses. He slid a hand inside the lapels of her robe and around her back to press her closer. Her skin felt like the softest silk, and he felt her tremble in his arms.

She groaned when he broke the kiss, her fabulous blue eyes unconsciously pleading for more as they met his. 'Trust me, Sally,' he murmured. 'It gets better.' And he turned her slender body so she was lying across his thighs, his hand moving from her back to caress one luscious breast, his thumb and finger rolling and plucking the perfect rosebud peak. She watched him with wide, almost innocent eyes, and squirmed in his arms.

'You like that?' he murmured, and delivered the same treatment to her other breast, parting her robe still further. 'Let me look at you, Sally,' he demanded huskily. 'All of you.' She was perfection, and he ached to see her completely naked.

Sally did not know what had hit her. All she knew was that the sensations swirling around inside her were new and wonderful, and the man staring down at her was responsible. His husky-toned request vibrated deep in her body, and she could feel herself becoming damp with desire. She had never been naked in front of a man before, but suddenly she'd lost all her inhibitions.

Later she would blame it on the wine and exhaustion, but at this moment she had never felt more vibrantly alive in her life.

'Yes…' she breathed, and he untied the belt at her waist and pushed the robe off her slender shoulders.

In a dreamlike trance her eyes settled on his ruggedly attractive face and she saw the dark stain spread across his high cheekbones, the gold flame of desire in his night-black eyes, as he studied her naked body with an intensity that made the blood race faster though her veins. His strong hand slowly caressed her throat, her breasts, followed the indentation of her waist, traced the curve of her hip and moved over her flat belly.

'You are perfect…more beautiful than I ever imagined,' he rasped.

Flattered, but aching with a need she had never felt before, Sally moved her hand from his shoulder to slip it beneath the open neck of his shirt, her fingers tracing the curling black hair shadowing his chest that had tempted her when he'd walked in the door earlier. She felt the fast pounding of his heart beneath her palm and gloried in the knowledge that she could do this to him.

'Oh, yes…' he groaned when she touched him.

His dark head bent and her lips parted in eager anticipation, but his head had dropped lower, and suddenly his mouth closed over one pert nipple, teeth biting gently, then lips suckling hard, as his long fingers tangled in the soft curls at the juncture of her thighs.

Sensation upon sensation sent shock waves crashing through her body, igniting a blazing heat that drove her wild, and she responded with an untutored intensity that would shock her when she recalled it later. She grasped his shirt and pulled it apart, unaware of the buttons flying off, and let her hands roam freely over his magnificent bronzed chest, glorying in the feel of his firm flesh, her fingers luxuriating in the soft mat of body hair, her nails finding and scraping over his small, pebble-like masculine nipples.

Zac growled deep in his throat, and, pulling back, he swept her up in his arms and navigated the few stairs to the bedroom area. His great body tense, he flicked the robe right off her body and laid her down on the bed.

Breathless and dizzy with an excitement she had never experienced before, Sally watched him with desire-glazed eyes. He kicked off his shoes, removed his shirt and stepped out of his pants, his dark eyes never leaving her naked body.

Sally could only gaze in awe at his magnificent golden-toned physique.

He was unashamedly and blatantly masculine, with wide shoulders and a broad, muscular chest. The body hair that so fascinated her fanned out over his masculine nipples and arrowed down over a hard flat stomach. A shocked gasp escaped her as he shed his silk boxers and she realised he was massively erect. A tide of red swept up her cheeks and she dropped her eyes, but his powerful muscled thighs and long legs did nothing to stop the blush, and for a second she was afraid.

She had a brief moment of clarity, and could not believe what she had allowed to happen. But as if sensing her reaction, Zac leant forward and placed a hand either side of her, his body not touching hers. Gently he brushed his lips across her forehead, the soft curve of her cheek, and finally closed them over her mouth, stifling any protest she might have made. And the moment was gone, lost in the magic of his kiss.

He raised his head, his smouldering black eyes sweeping over her slender frame in avid fascination. Then, as if she were a sculpture, his hands began to shape her body, his long fingers discovering every curve and crevasse, teasing her flesh in a way that made her insides shake. She stretched and turned at his bidding, and for the first time in her life she abandoned every restraint she had put on herself for years and gloried in her womanhood.

He cupped her breasts, squeezing them together and nipping the rigid tips between his long fingers. A helpless moan escaped her. She was totally overwhelmed by the power of what she was feeling, delirious with the pleasure he gave.

'You *really* like that?' He grinned.

Sally nodded her head, incapable of speech, and grasped his arm, urging him to join her on the bed. He stretched out beside her, one hand resting on her quivering stomach, the other smoothing a few silken strands of hair back from her face.

His hand curved around her waist and urged her closer to his side. The heat and the musky male scent of him tantalised her nostrils, and she felt the hard length of his arousal pressing against her thigh. Amazingly she wasn't afraid, but excited beyond reason. All she could think was that this magnificent man wanted her, and her head whirled as sensation after sensation arrowed through her body.

'Tell me what else you like, Sally,' he rasped huskily.

His hands were everywhere, and she looked at him, her whole body a quivering mass of feelings. 'You,' she said mindlessly, her brain turned to mush by sex.

His surveyed her with those smouldering eyes, one hand stroking over the flat plain of her stomach to settle at the juncture of her thighs and ease her legs apart, before his head dropped and his mouth covered a rigid nipple, suckling and tantalising yet again, until she didn't think she could bear it. Then Zac lifted his head, and his hard mouth covered her swollen lips.

Her slender arms dropped to curve around his broad back, her hands sliding down to stroke his hard buttocks before tracing up the line of his spine to curve around his broad shoulders, and finally reaching up to tangle in the thick black hair of his head.

She closed her eyes, shuddering in ecstasy at the feel of his hair-roughened chest against her acutely sensitised breasts. His tongue flicked evocatively around the outline of her lips and then thrust into her mouth as he kissed her with a hard, possessive passion, and her own tongue swirled round his in wild response.

His long fingers threaded thought the red curls at the apex of her thighs to find the velvet lips that guarded the hot, moist centre of her femininity, stroking over the tiny pleasure-point concealed there with unerring accuracy. She moaned and writhed beneath him, aching for more, her nails sinking into his flesh.

His mouth covered the pulse-point that beat frantically in her neck, and she turned her head to allow him easier access.

'You want this…' he growled against her throat.

She opened her eyes, and was just turning her head back to agree, white-hot and wanting, when she caught a glimpse of their naked bodies, erotically entwined, in the mirrored doors of the wardrobe…

To Sally it was like a douche of ice water on her overheated body, and she froze.

'No. Oh, no!' she cried, and shoved hard at Zac's shoulders, catching him by surprise.

He reared back.

'No?' he grated, and she caught the look of shock on his darkly flushed face—or was it pain?

She didn't wait to decide, and scrambled off the bed, picking up her robe. With legs that trembled she stumbled down to the living area, pulling it on. She fastened the belt around her waist so tight it hurt, her heart pounding like a sledgehammer in her chest.

The image in the mirror of naked lovers was indelibly printed on her mind. No, not lovers. A couple indulging in sex, she amended. She had barely recognised herself, wantonly splayed beneath Zac's great body. But she had been instantly reminded of where she was: her dad's old love-nest.

She was not like her dad and never would be, she vowed.

The first day she had moved in she had removed the mirror that had hung above the bed, but the mirrored wardrobe doors had been a timely reminder. How many young women had her dad seduced in the exact same place? But she wasn't about to make the same mistake with Zac Delucca...

Oh, no! In her panic she had forgotten about him for a moment, but not any more. Her body ached with the unfamiliar feeling of sexual frustration. What on earth was she going to say to him?

Painfully aroused and burning up with rage, Zac lay on his stomach and counted to a hundred—a technique he had learned in the ring. A fighter who let his anger get the better of him and lost control rarely won. That was the first piece of advice Marco, his manager at the time, had ever given him. And he knew if he lost control with his red-headed temptress he was liable to shake her until she rattled.

She had said no. Sally had actually said no. He was aware it was a woman's prerogative to change her mind, and he appreciated that, but he had never had a woman say no to him in bed before.

The little witch had been with him all the way. He could still feel the sting of her nails on his back. She had led him right to the edge and then slammed on the brakes. Pride and other darker emotions had him clenching his fists. No one got away with playing games with him. He rolled off the bed and pulled on his clothes, then descended the few steps to the living area, where the object of his fury and frustration stood, head bowed.

The footsteps on the wooden floor alerted Sally, and slowly she turned round. He was dressed—

well, almost; his shirt was open to where he had tucked it in his jeans, the buttons gone. A guilty tide of red swept over her face as the memory of pulling his shirt apart flashed in her mind.

'Have you any reasonable explanation?' he asked scathingly, and, not waiting for a reply, continued, 'Or is it a habit of yours to encourage a man, tell him you want him, rip off his shirt, strip naked and get into bed with him before running from the room?' he demanded with biting sarcasm.

She raised her head. Not a muscle flickered in the hard bronzed mask of his face, but his dark eyes blazed with a violent anger. She took a step back, suddenly afraid, very afraid, as it hit her just exactly what she had done...

'No...' she murmured. The air was heavy with tension, as was the man watching her she realised, his hands clenching and unclenching at his sides.

'You have a right to look afraid,' he snarled, and stepped towards her, his tall body looming over her. He grasped her chin and tilted her head back. 'Some women like to tease, but you take it too far. Consider yourself lucky it was me you tried your trick on. The next man might not have my control, and then you will get a hell of a lot more than you bargained for.'

A tremor slithered down her spine, and he noticed.

'You were not immune. You were with me all the way. Even now you tremble.'

Catching her hand, he forced it down to his thighs. She was shocked to find he was still aroused, and to her shame involuntarily her fingers flexed on his erection.

'Not too late to change your mind—after all, it is a woman's prerogative,' he drawled derisively.

'No... No!' she cried, snatching her hand free and stepping back, her face a fiery-red. She wondered how she could have been so stupid. Such a push-over.

'One no is enough. I get the message.'

'Fine,' she said, and her casual response, the use of the damn word *fine* enraged him further. For a timeless second Zac let the mask slip, and if looks could kill, she would have breathed her last by now.

Sally knew she wasn't blameless, and he had some justification for being furious, but with exhaustion overtaking her all she wanted to do was get rid of him and forget tonight had ever happened.

Maybe she did owe him an apology. Years ago her mum had told her the best way to defuse an argument was to say sorry. Whether you thought you were right or not did not matter, because it was very hard to continue arguing with someone who was saying sorry.

Well, Zac was bristling with anger. It was worth a try. Bravely she looked up into his hard face. 'I'm sorry for how I behaved, and I apologise if you feel you have been cheated,' she offered. 'But may I point out I did not invite you here? I told you I was tired, and I asked you to go, but you talked your way round me.' She made a futile gesture with her hands. 'You are like a tank, rolling over any sign of opposition. You are too much for me, and I want you to leave now.'

'My size intimidates you?' Zac demanded.

'No,' Sally snapped. She had told him a bit of the truth, and his continuing presence in her apartment was frustrating, so she told him the rest.

'You are just too much *everything*—too wealthy, too arrogant and too stubborn to leave when asked. And I don't like you. Apart from anything else you bought Westwold, which makes you an arms dealer, which to me is a despicable business.'

'That is rich, coming from you.' His tone was bitingly cynical. 'Daddy's little golden girl, who has never done a day's work in her life. The arms business has supported you very nicely—it paid for this apartment your father gave you, for starters. Perhaps I should have arrived with a jewellery box instead of a cool box. No doubt the outcome would have been different.'

The insult enraged Sally. It was bad enough that her father had told Zac he had given her the apartment, and she could not deny it, but he obviously had not told Zac she worked—hence his summing up of her character as an idle little rich girl. Knowing her dad, it had probably stroked his ego to come across as the generous father.

'Yes, you are right. Silly me,' she said, with a heavy irony which was wasted on Zac Delucca. She could explain, but she owed this arrogant bastard nothing. Crossing to the coffee table, she picked up the cool box. 'Now we know what we think of each other, take this and get out.'

Zac studied her for a moment, his lithe muscular body tense. 'Keep it as a gift from me,' he drawled tightly, and she noticed the way a little muscle jerked in his cheek. 'A cool box is quite appropriate for a woman who blows hot and cold like you. When you're lying in bed, burning up and remembering what you have missed, stick your beautiful head in it.'

Her brows shot up, and, holding her anger in, she said acidly, 'In your dreams—but certainly not in mine.'

His hand snaked out and tangled in her hair, jerking her towards him. 'Do you know, Miss Paxton…' his smile was chilling '…I'm minded to prove you wrong.'

She tried to pull her head away from him, but his hand tightened, and she stared up at him, her blue eyes spitting flames. Suddenly she was aware of the sexual violence emanating from every line of his powerful body.

'Don't even try,' she snapped.

He raised one dark brow. 'Big mistake, Sally,' he drawled mockingly. 'Did your mother never tell you you should never challenge an angry man?' He snaked a long arm around her waist to pull her hard against him.

'Let me go.' There was a brief silence as his eyes narrowed on her mouth. She was stiff with anger, and suddenly very afraid. 'I said let go of me.'

Zac gave her another chilling smile. 'I will, but first here is something to remember me by.'

Her eyes widened as his head bent and his mouth ravaged hers in a kiss of savage passion.

When he finally let her go she was gasping for breath and her legs were trembling. 'You... You...' she spluttered, livid with rage—and something more she refused to acknowledge.

He placed a finger over her lips. 'Save it. I am leaving and I won't be back.' He stared at her for a moment, a look of icy contempt in his hard eyes. 'Shame... It could have been good—but I am not into playing games, and you are nothing but a spoilt little tease.' He shrugged his broad shoulders and turned and walked to the door.

Sally shivered and collapsed onto the sofa. Her head fell back against the cushions, a long, sad sigh escaping her. All her emotional energy was spent worrying about her mother, and she had none to waste on Zac. A man born with a silver spoon in his mouth and accustomed to wealth and power, who expected women to simply fall at his feet, was not for her.

She did not see Zac glance back, nor the frown that creased his broad brow. She only heard the closing of the door as he left.

Zac walked into the elevator and pressed the button for the ground floor. He had caught the same expression of sadness on Sally's face just now, as he'd left, as he had when they'd first met. For a second he was tempted to go to her. Then common sense prevailed.

Over the weekend he and Raffe had discovered how her father had been robbing the company for years. Today they had added up the cost, and it was well over a million. He had told Raffe he would deal with Paxton in his own time, and had sent Raffe back to the head office in Rome—mainly because of Sally. He had behaved like a stupid lovesick teenager, soft in the head and hard everywhere else.

Well, no more… He punched the wall of the lift, and barely bruised his knuckles. Never had a woman led him on and then turned him down so callously, and he would make damn sure it never happened again.

In the morning he would face Nigel Paxton with the evidence of the man's fraud, and from now on he would stick to the sophisticated ladies who mixed in his circles and played the game by his rules. In fact, he would make a dinner date with Margot, a lawyer who had made it obvious she would be up for anything—which, ironically, was why he hadn't bothered before. But tomorrow he would, and he'd be fine…

CHAPTER SIX

THE restaurant was exclusive and very expensive and the latest fashionable place to eat. Sally looked at her companion across the table and smiled. Al was just what she needed. She had dressed carefully for their date in an effort to cheer herself up. The scarlet dress she was wearing had shoestring straps, a fitted bodice with a wide soft leather belt, and a short, gently flaring skirt. She had swept her hair up in a loose pile of curls on top of her head, mainly to keep cool in the hot weather London was experiencing. Al had taken one look at her and told her she looked fabulous, which had done a lot for her confidence, and then they had caught a taxi to the restaurant so Al could have a drink.

He had spent the last ten minutes waxing lyrical about a girl he had met last weekend at a house party given by one of his father's clients on an estate in Northumberland. Apparently, she was the owner's daughter, and it was she who had turned him down for dinner tonight.

Sally pointed out if the girl lived in Northumberland it was hardly surprising. It was the other end of England, and not everyone owned a private Piper plane like his dad. If he was keen, he should fly up north to see her again.

'Of course—why didn't I think of that?' Al laughed. 'You are so bright, Sally. Your advice is always good.'

The wine waiter arrived with an excellent bottle of Chardonnay and filled their glasses, and they drank a toast to each other. Then Al began regaling her with tall tales of his South American trip, making her laugh.

After a delicious main course they were soon waiting for their dessert, and Al reached across the table and took her hand in his, his blue eyes suddenly serious.

'Enough about me, old girl. Apart from your work, you have avoided telling me anything about what is going on in your life. What is really bothering you?'

'Not me.' She sighed. 'My mother.' It was such a relief to talk to someone who understood, and softly she told him about her mum's accident and prognosis. He lifted her hand and pressed a soft kiss on the back.

'Sorry, Sally. It must be hard. If there is anything I can do for you, anything at all, you only have to ask—you know that. You have my number, just call.'

She lifted moisture-filled eyes to his. 'I know, Al, and thanks.' She tried to smile. 'And I might take you up on that one day.'

Zac Delucca, seated in an intimate booth at the rear of the restaurant, had been enjoying his dinner with Margot, the intelligent thirty-something company lawyer he had met when negotiating on an apartment block he had bought in London a few years ago. He'd been pleasantly contemplating how the evening would end when his attention had been drawn to a couple entering the restaurant.

It was Sally Paxton, wearing a low-cut red silk dress that fitted her like a glove, emphasising her tiny waist, the curve of her hips, then flaring out provocatively as she walked. It ended a good three inches above her knees. The colour should have clashed with her hair, but didn't, and the same sexy red high-heeled sandals he had noticed the first time he saw her enhanced her shapely legs.

She was hanging onto her so-called friend Al's arm, and Zac could not keep his eyes off her.

He had watched them sit down at a table near the entrance, a simmering anger engulfing him.

He had barely listened to Margot's conversation, simply nodding his head occasionally, or slotting in a yes or a no. His whole attention was focused on the younger couple. Sally Paxton had turned him down in the most brutal way possible, and now she was smiling, laughing, holding Al's hand and looking into his eyes as though he was her soul mate.

He had seen enough, and he had changed his mind again… His interest in Margot, fleeting at best, was killed stone-dead. He signalled for the bill, paid it and got to his feet.

'You are in a rush? We have not had dessert or coffee.'

He had almost forgotten his companion, and glanced down at her.

She smiled as she stood up to join him, and clung to his arm, a blatant invitation in her eyes. 'But we can have coffee at my place.'

He gave her the briefest of smiles and said nothing. She was going to be disappointed…

Sally glanced up as the waiter arrived with their dessert, and the emotional moment was gone. 'This looks positively sinful!' She smiled, eyeing the small mountain of profiteroles covered in chocolate sauce and surrounded by cream…

'Don't look now, but a man you know who

probably *is* sinful is heading this way with a stunning woman on his arm,' Al said quietly.

'Who?' She glanced enquiringly at Al, but before he could answer, a familiar tall dark-headed man stopped at their table.

'Hello, Al—and Sally. Nice to see you again.'

Al replied sociably, but the deep, dark voice had sent every nerve in Sally's body jangling.

She looked up. Zac was standing by the table, wide-shouldered, lean-hipped and long-limbed. He was wearing a perfectly tailored grey suit, a white shirt and matching tie, and he looked fabulous.

Sally was struck dumb as his dark eyes stared down into hers, and a vivid image of herself lying naked beneath him flashed in her head. She glanced to his companion and fought back the blush that threatened. The beautiful raven-haired woman clinging to his arm was almost as impressive as Zac. Tall and slender, she wore her lime-green designer gown like a model.

She probably *was* a model, Sally thought, and her brief moment of embarrassment was gone.

She had been right to say no last night to Zac Delucca. His women were as interchangeable as his shirts, and she told herself she had had a lucky escape. But she was slightly surprised that he had bothered to stop and say hello... When he'd left her apartment his contemptuous farewell had been very final.

'Enjoying your meal, Sally?'

There it was again, the seductive voice, but it was wasted on her.

She glanced up, saw the smile on his attractive face and noted that it did not reach his hard dark eyes. 'I was,' she said, with biting sarcasm.

Zac Delucca stared at her, stunned by the implied insult. Rage such as he had never felt before swept through him, and his hard black eyes raked furiously over her. He noted her exquisite face, carefully made up, and the silken red hair piled on top of her head in a mass of curls, enhancing the long line of her neck and the low neckline of her dress, which revealed a generous glimpse of her firm white breasts No one insulted him publicly and got away with it. Very few would dare. Yet this redheaded Jezebel took delight in taking potshots at him. Well, not any more. Last night she had been naked in his arms, and she would be again, he vowed.

He had confronted Nigel Paxton this morning with his fraudulent actions, and listened to the man's paltry defence. Zac had told him he was considering police action, but he wasn't… Being tied up in a court case was not Zac's idea of fun, and admitting someone had managed to cheat him was not good for business, but he had not given Paxton his final decision nor fired him yet. He had thought to let him stew for a day or two—it was the least he deserved—and now Zac was glad he had as a much more personal solution to the problem formed in his mind.

Sally saw the fury in Zac's face for a split second and she held her breath as the silence lengthened, her heart beating faster in her breast. Maybe she had gone too far. It was not like her to be deliberately impolite.

Finally, he smiled, a humourless twist of his chiselled lips, his dark eyes clashing with hers. 'Ever the tease, Sally,' he drawled sardonically. 'Enjoy the rest of your meal.' And he was gone.

Zac's subtle reminder of last night had brought a pink tinge to her cheeks, and she heaved a sigh of relief and began to relax again as the couple left the restaurant.

'What was all that about?' Al asked. 'Delucca was furious, and I certainly wouldn't ever want to be on the receiving end of the look you just got.'

'Nothing. Now, can I enjoy my dessert in peace, please?'

'Yes, but I have warned you once about Delucca. He is really not a man to fool around with, and certainly not the type to insult.'

'Al, don't worry—I am never going to see the man again, and he certainly will not want to see me.' She grinned. 'Trust me, his ego is as big as his bank balance.'

'My point exactly,' Al cut in. 'Nobody insults a man like that and gets away with it. Take it from me as a man. I recognise the signs. He was angry, but on a primitive level he wants you badly, and I would hate to see you get hurt. So beware.'

The telephone was ringing as she entered her apartment a couple of hours later. They had finished their meal, and then, as it was such a lovely summer night, Al had walked her home.

'Yes?' she answered.

'Is he with you?'

It was Zac, and she could not believe the nerve of the man. 'No—not that it is any of your business. And do not ring this—'

'This *is* business,' he cut in. 'Have you talked to your father today?' he demanded.

'My father? No.' The question surprised her, and instead of hanging up on him she listened.

'Then I suggest you do—soon. I will be round at eight tomorrow night…'

'Now, wait a damn minute—' But this time it was Zac who hung up on her…

Sally slowly replaced the receiver, a puzzled frown creasing her brow. Why would Zac Delucca tell her to call her dad? It didn't make sense. Well, she wasn't calling her dad tonight. It was too late, and he was probably in bed with his mistress. Given Zac's brief call, he was probably doing the same with Margot…

On Wednesday morning, after a restless night, Sally was running late. She had stripped the bed and changed the linen after Zac had left on Monday, yet for some reason she imagined she could still smell the scent of him whenever she tried to sleep. Maybe it was the pillows, she reasoned as she dashed out to go to work. She would buy two new ones, she decided, and any thought of calling her father was forgotten.

Usually Sally stayed in the museum for lunch, but today, after ringing her mum to check she was all right as she did every day, she went out shopping. She bought two pillows, and then stocked up in a grocery store with some essentials: fresh bread, milk and a few ready meals. Her weekends with her mother did not leave her with much time for shopping, and she rarely bothered to cook in the evenings any more.

She dashed into her apartment building that evening as the storm clouds that had been gathering for the past few hours finally broke in a deluge of rain.

'You just made it in time, Miss Paxton.' The

doorman grinned. 'So much for the heat wave—it lasted all of two weeks.'

'This is England, remember?' Sally quipped, and headed for the elevator.

A few minutes later she entered her apartment to the sound of the telephone ringing. Her hands were full of shopping, so she placed the pillows and the groceries on the kitchen bench, and then lifted the receiver from the wall.

'Where have you been? I have been ringing you since yesterday, and you were out last night.' It was her father.

'Even I have the occasional date, and I go to work, remember? And when I'm not working I visit my mother—your wife. I have tried to call you for weeks to get you to visit her, with no success. So now you know how it feels.'

'Yes, yes, I know all that. But listen to me. This is important. Has Zac Delucca rung you?'

'Why would he ring me? I barely know the man,' she said, suddenly tense as she belatedly remembered Zac calling her last night and suggesting she speak to her father.

'You know him well enough—you had lunch with him on Friday.'

'That was a one-off and never to be repeated,' she said adamantly.

'Don't be so hasty to dismiss him, Sally,

darling, because I gave him your telephone number yesterday.'

'You had no right,' she shot back, but as the hateful man had already known her number, there was no point arguing the issue.

'Never mind that now, and listen. The man is a ruthless bastard. His employees are all terrified of him—he is noted for paring the workforce to the bone whenever he takes over a company, or closing it down completely and selling the assets. So if you want me to keep my career, I need him on my side.'

'Surely you can do that yourself? In every other aspect of your life you are a waste of space, but even I accept you are good at your job,' Sally said dryly.

'I have tried, but the man trusts no one except that sidekick of his, Costa, and Costa found out I'd overlooked a rule or two and told the boss. I had an awkward meeting with Delucca yesterday, and in the process I suggested he might like to check me out through you, so promise me if he calls you will be nice to him.'

Her father was worried about something. She recognised the blustering tone of his voice and re-membered she had seen a hint of it the other day in the office, when Zac Delucca arrived.

Her dad had admitted to 'overlooking' a rule or two—probably caught with his pants down with his secretary again, she thought bitterly. Most businesses had strict rules about relationships in the workplace, and the majority of people had the sense to keep their personal lives out of the office, but her father had never made that distinction.

'I know your opinion of me, but think of your mother. I've already told Delucca she is paralysed and in a very expensive nursing home, hoping for the sympathy vote. All I want you to do is back me up if he calls you—though time is running out.' He sighed. 'I have another meeting with him tomorrow morning.'

'I'll back you up if he calls,' she said noncommittally.

She had no qualms about lying to her father, and she had no intention of telling him Delucca had already called, but suddenly she saw a way to make her beloved mother happy.

'On one condition—you give me your solemn promise to visit Mum with me at the weekend. I'll pick you up and book you into the hotel I use, and just for once you will stay the *whole* weekend.'

'It's a deal. I promise,' he said, relief evident in his tone. 'But try to remember you are a beautiful woman, and Delucca is a very eligible man. He took you out to lunch, so he must have fancied you. If you play your cards right you could do both of us a lot of good.'

'You, maybe. As for me, I think you are a despicable excuse for a man. Heaven knows why Mum loves you, because I certainly don't,' Sally said, and hung up.

Automatically she unpacked her shopping and put the food in the fridge. She carried the pillows across to the bed, and, after stripping off the pillowcases, changed the old for new. Then, taking her keys, she left the apartment and pushed the old pillows down the waste chute, at the same time wishing she could push Zac so easily from her mind.

She was going to have to talk to him. She would do anything to make her mum happy, and if that included facing Zac again and backing up her dad simply to get him to visit his wife, she would do it.

Sally returned to her apartment and closed the door. Zac had said he would be here at eight. She glanced at her watch. It was already seven. She crossed to her wardrobe, and, kicking off her shoes, placed them in the cupboard. She took out a well-washed pink velour lounging suit—the comfortable outfit she usually wore when she got home in the evening—and slipped her bare feet into flat furry pink mules; she refused to dress any differently from any other evening. She headed for the bathroom. After a quick shower she bundled her day clothes into the wash basket and slipped on clean underwear and the pink suit. Then, squaring her shoulders, she zipped up the top.

She wasn't out to impress, she told herself, and, returning to the living room, she sat down on the sofa, picking up the remote and switching on the television.

Normality was what she was striving for, but without much success. Her stomach churned with nerves, and she could not concentrate on the screen, but she did not have to for long as the intercom sounded.

She crossed to the door, hit the button and listened, then answered, 'Yes.'

She waited by the door, and when the bell rang opened it.

Zac stood like a dark avenging angel, big and tall, his black hair plastered to his head by the rain, his broad shoulders fitting perfectly beneath a dark jacket that had not fared much better. Beneath it he wore a black cotton tee shirt and dark pleated pants.

'May I come in?' he asked with icy politeness, and the eyes that met hers were hard and cold.

'Good to see you did not fib your way in this time,' she said. It was the first thing that came into her head as her heart lurched at the sight of him. She made an exaggerated gesture with one slender arm. 'Be my guest.'

He pushed past her and she caught the slightest scent of his cologne—sandalwood, maybe. Whatever it was, it had a disturbing effect on her. Her stomach fluttered as if a thousand butterflies had taken up residence, and angrily she told herself not to be so stupid.

This was business. Zac had said so, and her father had told her he would check him out with her. The female on Zac's arm last night confirmed he had certainly moved on in the sexual stakes... Sally would bet her last cent the willowy model had not said no.

'Sarcasm does not become you, Sally.'

'How would you know? You don't know me,' she snapped angrily, following him into the living room. He had removed his wet jacket and was in the process of looping it over the small stair rail, his back to her.

Slowly he turned round and stared at her with narrowed eyes, his expression unreadable.

'Maybe not completely...' His eyes narrowed further, scanning her slender body with deliberate provocation and making her remember their last encounter here. 'But I am going to—very well...' His smile was chilling.

'Not in this lifetime,' she said, her temper rising, the image of him with his latest conquest still in the forefront of her mind.

He took a step towards her. 'You have spoken to your father?' he queried, his dark eyes fixed intently on her flushed face.

The mention of her dad was enough to make her tense, and it didn't help that, minus his jacket, the black cotton tee shirt Zac wore moulded every muscle of his broad chest. She tried to ignore his much superior height and strength, but the sheer physical impact of the man was enough to make her go weak at the knees. 'Yes, of course I have,' she said bravely, holding his gaze.

'And you think you have a choice?' he demanded, with a mocking lift of one dark eyebrow.

'I don't know what you mean.' And she didn't. Simply looking at the damn man turned her brain to jelly. Gathering every shred of control she possessed, she continued. 'All I know is my father called me and told me he had given you my phone number. I didn't bother to tell him you already knew it,' she slotted in sarcastically. 'Then he told me everything.'

'Everything? And you *still* think you have a choice?' he queried, his dark eyes holding her.

'Yes,' she declared emphatically. 'Apparently, you are renowned for cutting the workforce or closing a place down altogether when you take over a company, and he is worried about his job. He may not be much of a husband, but I can assure you my mother *is* in a private nursing home and he *does* pay the fees. Whatever else my dad is, he is a good accountant. In fact, I don't know why you bothered coming here. We could just as easily have had this conversation over the telephone.'

Dark eyes full of contempt held hers for a long tense moment. 'You amaze me,' he finally drawled, and a frisson of alarm ran down her spine as his face darkened thunderously. 'You really don't give a damn.'

Pride made her face him, but inside she was shaking and her legs threatened to give way. 'If you are referring to my father…not particularly,' she responded, and she was not about to explain why. 'Now, if there is nothing more, I would like you to leave.'

Not waiting for his response, she turned and crossed to the sofa. Picking up the remote control, she switched off the television. She needed to do something to escape Zac's overpowering physical presence, and just prayed he would go—before her legs gave way beneath her and she collapsed in a heap at his feet.

'There is something more,' he said bitingly, turning his black head with chilling slowness to look at her with hard dark eyes. 'A lot more,' he added, walking towards her. 'The not inconsiderable sum of over one million pounds, stolen from the company, and how you can continue to live the way you do with your father in prison.'

CHAPTER SEVEN

PRIDE held Sally's head high, though the mention of a million pounds and prison had shocked her to the core. Her father was a fool over women, but she had never thought he was a thief. But then she had no idea to what depths he could sink in pursuit of his sybaritic lifestyle. She wouldn't put anything past him…

'Perfectly,' she answered Zac's question. 'Contrary to what you believe, my farther does not give me a penny and nor would I want him to. I can't stand him. He is everything I loathe in a man—a chauvinistic, womanising, unfaithful creep. Unfortunately, my mother loves him, and I love my mother, so I am obliged to be civil to him but that is all. I would not throw him a lifebelt if he was drowning, so whatever he has done is of no consequence to me,' she declared, letting all her anger and bitterness at her father spill out. 'I have taken care of myself for years now, and will continue to do so.'

'How?' His upper lip curled in a sneer. 'On your back?'

Her hand shot out and slapped his arrogant face. 'How dare you?' she spat, and hysterical laughter bubbled up inside her. She sounded like an outraged virgin...which she was.

His head jerked back in surprise, and before she knew what was happening he caught her shoulders and dragged her towards him.

'No one strikes me and gets away with it,' he grated through his teeth. 'Consider yourself lucky. If you were a man I'd have knocked you cold by now.' His dark eyes leaping with barely controlled rage, he added with deadly emphasis, 'But there are alternatives.'

Sally's pulse raced and she began to panic, seeing the menace and the threat of violence in his body. Frantically, she lashed out and tried to punch him, but his hands slipped down her back, pinioning her arms at her sides. His dark head bent and his mouth caught hers to inflict its own powerful method of retaliation.

She tried to twist her head away from his ruthless searching mouth, but Zac was stronger, and he kept her trapped against him, unable to escape the vengeful dominance of his savage kiss.

When he finally stopped ravaging her mouth she was left gasping for breath, her legs like rubber.

Still held against him, she could feel the heavy thud of his heart even as her own raced. Then something strange happened. Their eyes met and fused, and her heart leapt crazily at the predatory sexual awareness in his. She stared, wide-eyed, and to her shame it wasn't disgust that made her tremble but the heat of arousal curling in her pelvis.

A fierce tension arced in the air between them. How did he manage to affect her like this? His touch was like being struck by lightning, igniting a flame inside her every time he came near her. Mortified by her own weakness, with a terrific effort of will she made herself rigid in his hold. But her control was not needed. As she watched his expression changed from primitive male aggression to one of icy control…he was every inch the hard-faced captain of industry once more.

His arms dropped to his sides and she was free, but she didn't trust her legs to support her if she moved. Then he spoke.

'So, Miss Paxton, back to business. How do you intend to honour the debt of one million pounds plus that your father embezzled from Westwold?' he demanded, his cold, black eyes holding hers.

'I don't have to,' she said, breathing fast. 'It is not my debt.'

'True, but much as you seem to dislike your father, and insist you do not need his money, apparently—as you confirmed—your mother is in an expensive nursing home and she does. Unless, of course, you earn enough to keep her as well as yourself.'

He raised a brow and took a step back, his gaze raking over her from top to toe, assessing her worth as if she was a slave on the block.

'You are certainly beautiful enough on the outside, with all the attributes a man could want.' He eyed her comprehensively again. 'But you might have to work on your technique if the fiasco between us the other night was typical of your bedside manner.'

Sally stared in shock and outrage as the full import of his words sank in. Then her face paled to a deathly white as in her head flashed an image of her mother in bed, her once glorious red hair now a faded grey, her body half-paralysed. She had suffered more than any human being should have to endure, and no matter what Sally thought of her dad, she knew it would break her mother's heart completely if her husband was branded a thief and sent to prison. She could not let it happen, and she could not deprive her mother of the care and comfort of the nursing home for whatever amount of time she had left.

Sally searched Zac's harshly controlled features as if she had never seen him before. He had everything—looks, wealth and power—and he used it ruthlessly, looking down on lesser mortals like some pagan god.

Suddenly she was fed up and bristling with anger. She had always thought that a man who was dependent on the female members of his family to protect his honour didn't have much of that commodity to start with. Yet here she was, she thought furiously, an intelligent, hardworking adult female, put in this invidious position by two men: her father, a spineless jerk, and Zac Delucca, a titan among men but with a positively medieval attitude.

'For your information—' she eyed him with contempt '—I have a full-time job in a museum, and while I am quite happy with what I earn, museums are not noted for extravagant salaries. So, no, at the moment I could not pay the nursing home fees,' she told him bluntly, while silently racking her brain for a solution if her feckless father really was in deep trouble.

She had very little savings, and she spent any spare cash she had on her mother. Paying for accommodation every weekend to be near her was not cheap, but if she managed to sell her apartment she could use the money she gained to pay for her mum and rent somewhere else. So far she had received one ridiculously low offer from a property developer, which she had refused, but now she would accept it, she decided.

'But if you give me time a month or so I could afford to support my mum.' It suddenly occurred to her that her dad could do the same—sell his gran-diose apartment and pay Delucca back. 'And if you drop the charges against Dad between him and I we could almost certainly pay you back.' She had to think positive. Anything else was too degrading.

'Interesting, but no. Your father has stolen from the company for years, and he has run out of time.'

For a defeated second it occurred to her that if her mother died quickly the problem would disap-pear. 'Oh, my God,' she groaned, despising herself for the horrific thought.

Zac took her chin between a finger and thumb and tilted her head up to face him.

'Praying will not help you, Sally, but I might!' His heavy-lidded eyes glinted with a calculating light. 'I could be persuaded, with the right encour-agement, to accept the monetary loss and refrain from charging your father with theft and so keep him out of prison.'

His hand slipped from her chin to curve around her throat, and a strong arm closed around her waist to pull her into contact with his long, hard body. There was no mistaking his meaning.

'If you are really good I will allow him to draw

his present salary—in a more menial position, of course—until he reaches the retirement age of sixty, in twelve months, and I will also allow him to keep his generous pension, both of which he would forfeit if found guilty of fraud. With the money he has stolen it should be more than enough to allow him to fulfil his commitment to his wife.'

The blood drained from her face, and she was trembling with a mixture of fear and fury at his insulting proposal. 'You bastard!' Her blue eyes flashed at him.

'Such language for a lady—you do surprise me, Sally,' he mocked. 'And I am not, in the true sense of the word. My parents are long dead, but they *were* married when I was born.'

'And I am not some wh-whore to—to—to… do…' She stuttered to a stop—something she had not done since she was a child.

'I never actually said you were.' One dark brow arched sardonically, and a ruthless smile curved his sensuous mouth. 'What I am proposing is quite straightforward. In exchange for my saving your father from prison and allowing him to stay in my employ, you will become my mistress.'

She swallowed hard, her strained features reflecting her shock and confusion. Zac could not be serious…

In fact, he could be lying about her dad. But

then she remembered her father's conversation earlier. He had said he had 'overlooked' a rule or two, as if it was nothing to worry about. She had assumed it was to do with his penchant for bedding his secretaries. 'Is it true? About my father stealing?' she asked in a low voice.

'I do not lie, Sally. Your father has been swindling the company regularly for years, extremely cunningly. The amounts he took were small enough to be explained away as errors before I bought the company, but over a decade or more they became big enough to add up to a considerable sum. When Raffe took charge of the London headquarters he smelt a rat, but even he was not sure, and it took both of us to track where the money had gone,' he responded with a wry twist of his lips. 'So what is it going to be, Sally? Your father disgraced and broke, or you becoming my mistress?'

It was unthinkable. But deep down inside Sally knew he was telling her the truth. She also knew that for her mother's sake she could not let her dad go to prison.

'Why me?' she murmured to herself. Didn't she have enough to suffer, watching her mum dying? And now she had no choice but to agree to Zac's outrageous demand.

She wasn't an idiot, and not for a minute did she kid herself he was doing it for anything other than revenge. A million pounds was small change to him. And she was no financial expert, but, if her dad had been stealing for years, surely technically it was the previous owner who had lost most of the money, not Zac? But the blow to his ego she had dealt him by saying no on Monday, and then insulting him in public last night, were not things a man like Zac Delucca was going to forgive and forget in a hurry.

'Look at me.' His arm tightened around her waist and the hand at her throat slipped around the nape of her neck to tilt her head up to face him. 'You know why, Sally. I want you badly, and though you try your best to ignore the sexual chemistry between us you want me. If this is the only way to have you, then so be it.'

She had not realised she had spoken out loud, and she opened her mouth to deny his assumption. But his mouth had found hers, and, unlike their previous kiss, his tongue was gently outlining her lips and then probing into the warm interior of her mouth with a persuasive eroticism that totally enthralled her.

Desire and disgust fought for supremacy in her shattered mind. Desire won as a surging tide of excitement swept though her still shaken body. She must not let him know how easily he could affect her, she told herself, but involuntarily she leant against his hard frame, her pulse beginning to beat like a drum in her throat as she surrendered to his expert seduction of her senses.

'Has that helped you to decide, *cara mia?*' His husky chuckle sounded against her ear long, passion-filled moments later.

He knew he had won, Sally thought helplessly as she forced herself to struggle out of his arms. Her legs no longer capable of supporting her, she finally collapsed onto the sofa behind her.

Zac looked down at her, and she saw the knowing smile of masculine triumph curving his mobile mouth. He knew he could elicit a sensual response from her with humiliating ease, and his eyes challenged her to deny it…

She wanted to say no. She opened her mouth to do so—and closed it. Damn him to hell, she swore under her breath, and clasped her hands in her lap to stop them shaking. She stared down at them, unconsciously gnawing on her bottom lip, while her mind spun frantically as she sought for inspiration to escape what was virtually a hopeless position. Finally she took a long resigned breath, her decision made…

She would do anything for her mother, and if that meant saving the neck of her father by sleeping with Zac, she would do it. She glanced around the room, and the irony of the situation hit her.

How appropriate… Her dad's love-nest…and now hers…

A fatalistic calm swept over her, soothing her nerves and clearing her head. She was twenty-six next month, and with her father as an example she had no intention of ever marrying. As for falling in love, she only had to look at what it had done to her mother to dismiss the idea completely. Maybe it was time she took a lover, and, being brutally honest, she had no doubt Zac Delucca would be a magnificent one. She only had to remember the time she was naked in bed with him to know that. But pride and pride alone insisted that while accepting his offer she would do her utmost to remain unresponsive in his arms. A man of his ego would soon grow tired of a reluctant mistress…

'Your argument is very persuasive,' she conceded, and raising her head she caught the flicker of surprise in his dark eyes. 'I would have to be a fool to refuse what you are offering. So, yes, I agree to be your mistress—but with a few guidelines in place.'

'Guidelines?' he queried. 'Maybe your past lovers catered to your every whim, but I am not that type of man. I expect my woman to be available whenever and wherever I want her. No rules but mine apply. After all, in your case that is what I have already paid for.'

'Sorry, not possible,' she said with a shake of her head. She could be as businesslike as he was when she had to be. 'I have a degree in Ancient History and I work as a researcher at the British museum. My hours are nine to five-thirty, sometimes later, Monday to Friday. I spend every weekend visiting my mother at her nursing home in Devon, returning late on Sunday evening. The guidelines I was referring to are that on no account must my father discover the arrangement between us, and obviously not my mother either. It will be solely between us, and that you can come here any evening except Saturday and Sunday.'

Zac looked down at her pale, determined face and was stunned. He'd had no idea she was a graduate and held down a job at a prestigious museum. When she'd said 'museum' he had thought she was probably a receptionist at some commercial tourist attraction, like a house of horrors or a toy museum—there were plenty of them scattered around most major cities.

Blinded by lust the moment he set eyes on her, he had leapt to assumptions about her lifestyle with very little evidence and had misjudged her badly. She wasn't the spoiled, attention-seeking Daddy's darling he had thought her, and her dislike of the man was obviously one hundred percent genuine. The knowledge made Zac uneasy—more so when he realised she had actually taken his word against her father's regarding the theft with barely a quibble, and accepted his offer much more quickly than he had expected.

Then, cynically, he wondered if she was spinning him a line as he recalled the first time he'd met her, in the middle of a working day, elegant and immaculately dressed. Zac could recognise a designer gown when he saw one; he had paid for enough over the years.

'If what you say is true, Sally, then explain to me how you were free last Friday and looking as if you had just stepped out of *Vogue*,' he demanded.

'I have three designer garments for special occasions that I bought in a secondhand shop here in Kensington. All at least a couple of years out of date, and deposited there by the sort of woman you usually escort, who discard them after a season or sell them,' she said scathingly.

Zac flinched, reminded of his years in the orphanage, when the clothes he'd worn had all been secondhand, donated by the good citizens of the city.

'For months I have been researching the history of a collection of Egyptian artefacts that had been stored in the basement for years prior to the new extension of a current exhibition. It happened to preview to the press and dignitaries last Friday morning. My boss asked me to attend the opening to answer any historical queries that might arise, hence the dress. Then he gave me the afternoon off as he knew I wanted to visit my mother.'

Zac flinched again as he recognised the sadness she could not hide shimmering in her blue eyes. Then he wondered if he had imagined it as she raised her head.

Control tightened her exquisite features, and her blue gaze was cold as she continued, 'Unlike you, apparently a boss that terrifies his employees, my boss Charles is a kind, thoughtful man. The reason I was at Westwold was because I had hoped to persuade my father to come with me and visit mum that night or the next day. Unfortunately for me you arrived! Satisfied…?'

After feeling uneasy about the way he had treated her, by the time she'd finished speaking all he felt was anger. How did the little witch do it? Yet again she had managed to insult him twice, without even blinking an eye.

'Satisfied? My curiosity, yes, the rest of me, no. But I will be,' he drawled, and, reaching down, he caught her hand and drew her to her feet. 'I accept your guidelines, Sally Paxton, and now, as my mistress, you have to accept me.'

Surely he could not possibly mean that they should go to bed here and now?

A trickle of fear snaked down Sally's spine, and

she went hot and cold by turns. But she refused to give in to the emotion. Instead she pulled her hand from his, straightened her shoulders, looked him squarely in the eyes, her own eyes bleak, and simply said, 'Fine.'

The *fine* got to Zac; he knew she used the word when she didn't care one way or the other. Well, he was going to make her care, he vowed.

'Good. You can start by stripping off that outfit that covers you from head to toe,' he suggested. 'Or I will—the choice is yours.'

He meant it. He actually expected her to cold-bloodedly strip naked in front of him. Not content with virtually blackmailing her into being his mistress, he wanted to humiliate her as well.

Sally's cool control finally shattered. 'If I had a choice I'd never set eyes on you again,' she told him, eyes blazing. 'I hate you.'

'Hate is better than indifference.' He shrugged his broad shoulders. 'You agreed to be my mistress, and the only choice you have left is the one I just gave you, Sally.' His voice dropped to a low, menacing drawl. 'And if you don't make up your mind quickly I will do it for you.'

Swept along on a white-hot tide of burning rage, Sally unzipped her top and shrugged it off her shoulders, then slipped the pants down her hips and stepped out of them.

His dark eyes swept over her, and the hint of a smile tilted the corners of his mouth as he noted the white cotton knickers and sports bra. 'Very virginal—and we both know you are not. Just as well, because I prefer my women experienced, and wearing silk and lace or nothing at all.'

In a second of blinding clarity Sally saw her salvation. She was not mistress material, as he would quickly discover, and given his declared tastes Zac would not hang around long. Instead of trying to resist him in bed she should encourage him. The quicker she got it over with, the quicker he would be gone.

'As you wish.' She unfastened her bra and let it fall, then hesitated. Reminding herself he had seen it all, she gathered her courage and stripped off her briefs, and in a show of bravado straightened to her full height and flung her arms wide. 'What you see is what you get,' she said, and pirouetted on her toes.

But she did not complete the circle.

Zac gathered her up in full spin and strode over to the bed. Sweeping back the embroidered cotton cover, he dropped her so hard she bounced.

CHAPTER EIGHT

HE STOOD menacingly over her, blocking out most of the daylight that was left, and suddenly the anger that had got her this far deserted her. What was she thinking of? Had she taken leave of her senses? She couldn't do this…

'Don't even think about it,' he commanded.

He had read her mind. How did he do that? she wondered, and saw him take something from his pants pocket and drop it on the bedside table before whipping his tee shirt over his head and dropping it on the floor.

Helplessly, she stared up at him, her fascinated gaze taking in the masculine perfection of his great body, and the thin line of black hair arrowing down over the strong packed band of muscles over his ribcage and then lower, as he shrugged out of the rest of his clothes.

'There is no changing your mind this time, Sally,' he drawled with implacable determination in his tone.

She swallowed hard. Totally nude and aroused he was magnificent. He was also vastly experienced, and she felt hopelessly inadequate. With that thought came another. She suddenly realised she had no guarantee he would save her father.

'But what if you change yours?' she asked. 'How do I know you will honour your side of the deal?'

He tensed, his dark eyes seeking hers. 'Because we made a deal and I gave you my word. My word is my bond.'

She didn't question why, but she believed him—not that it stopped her nerves from leaping all over the place at the thought of what was about to happen, nor her adding, 'Even if you think I am really bad?'

'I certainly hope so. I rather like bad women.' Zac gave a low, husky chuckle and slid in beside her. Leaning up on one elbow, he let his gaze sweep leisurely over her long-legged curvaceous figure. She had a body made for sex, and he wondered why he had wasted so much time with tall, stick-thin women.

'Perfection,' he husked, and began to caress her with long light strokes, from her shoulders to her breasts, her narrow waist, the curve of her hips. He felt her tense, but he did not linger in any one spot, long fingers trailing over her flat stomach and down the length of her leg, then back up her other leg to circle her belly button, and higher to graze the tips of her breasts. He watched the hardening nipples with a hunger he refused to give in to… yet… He didn't want a passive lover; he wanted a passionate lover.

He saw her blue eyes widen, and the pupils expand and darken involuntarily. He heard her breathing quicken, heard the small whimpers of delight she could not control from her lushly parted lips, felt her small hand slip around his back and tentatively stroke up his spine. He had her, she was his, but he resisted the incredible urge to kiss her.

Instead he continued to caress her throat, and down the valley between her breasts. The tight nipples were pouting for his attention while his hand slid lower to the hidden valley between her thighs. Her legs parted for him, and it took every ounce of control he possessed not to take her there and then.

He pressed the heel of his hand on her soft mound and raised his head to look down at her beautiful face, flushed with arousal, and he made a husky-voiced promise. 'I am going to pleasure you more than any man has ever done before, Salmacis.'

Sally stared wildly up at Zac. He was torturing her, but it was an exquisite torture. The brushing, teasing softness of his fingers was driving her insane. She was hot and aching, and with a bravado she hadn't thought she was capable of she let her free hand sweep down over his chest and then lower, to touch his erection. She heard him groan, 'No…' and an impish smile curved her kiss-starved lips.

'Do you mean that?' she asked breathlessly, and with one finger traced the smooth, silken tip. Fascinated, she let her hand curl around the hard, pulsing length of him. Her fingers would not meet around the girth, but that did not stop her stroking down to the base and slowly retracing the path back up again.

'No…yes…' he groaned again, and, grasping her wrist, he pulled her hand up his body. 'Always the tease,' he breathed against her lips, and then, rearing up, he grasped her hands and pushed them above her head, to anchor them there with one of his as his mouth came crashing down on hers in a kiss of awesome passion.

She was pinned beneath him, and he took full advantage of her helpless state. With lips and tongue he teased and tantalised, sucking on the pulse beating madly in her throat and then moving lower to draw a rigid nipple into his mouth and suckle some more. Her back arched and she tried to free her wrists. But his clasp tightened as he kissed, nipped, stroked and licked every throbbing inch of her. His long fingers finally slipped between her thighs to dip into her moist core, finding and toying with the sensitive nub hiding there to devastating effect.

Crazy with excitement, she writhed beneath him as an incredible tension built and built inside her. Just when she thought she could take no more he let her hands free, and she moaned out loud as for a moment she quivered on the brink of some wondrous place she could barely imagine.

He reached across to the table, then grasped her hips and lifted her off the bed. She felt the tip of his shaft slide between her thighs. Involuntarily she wrapped her legs around his waist and her slender arms around his neck, to pull him to her, and her mouth opened beneath his with a white-hot hungry need her body recognised as he plunged into her.

She cried out with a pain she had not expected, and his great body stilled.

He looked into her eyes, his own black and burning like living coals of fire. 'You're a virgin.'

'Was…' she murmured distractedly, the acute stab of pain easing and the promise of exquisite pleasure returning as her body adjusted to the rigid fullness of him. She wriggled her hips and clasped her arms a little tighter around his neck.

'What are you doing?' Zac demanded, about to pull back, but she wrapped her legs even tighter around his waist.

'I don't know—I thought you did.' She gave him a wicked smile.

Zac grinned, then grimaced in an effort to still

his raging body. He looked into her incredible eyes, the pupils big and dark with sensual hunger, and yet humour lurked.

Something squeezed in his chest at the same time as her inner muscles clenched around him. He had never felt anything like it in his life. He caught her husky moans of pleasure in his mouth and began to move slowly. She was so tight he was afraid of hurting her, and, hanging on to his control by a thread, he pushed inch by inch into her sleek silken sheath and then slowly withdrew. Again and again he stroked into the honeyed depths, and only when he felt her whole body begin to convulse in the ultimate pleasure, and heard her keening cry, did his iron control break free. Helpless in the throes of a sensual storm, he plunged hard and fast to join her in an earth-shattering climax.

He rolled on to his back, carrying Sally with him, and held her close against his heaving chest. He had never known a woman like her. Her fabulous body was sinfully sexy, and so instantly responsive to his slightest touch. Usually for Zac sex was a relaxing exercise, with a like-minded woman, during which the sole aim was to make the right moves and lead to a satisfactory conclusion for both.

But with Sally it was a sensual feast—and fun… He couldn't believe she had been a virgin. He had never made love to a virgin in his life. He had always steered well clear of the innocent type. But now, in a totally proprietorial way, he found enormous satisfaction in knowing he had initiated the lovely Salmacis into the joys of sex, and also oddly protective.

'Are you all right, Sally?' he rasped a long moment later, when his breathing had slowed, and he smoothed the hair from her forehead with a hand that was not quite steady. She hadn't said a word—maybe he had hurt her. He had lost control at the end, and he was a big man with everything in proportion.

Suddenly it occurred to him why she had said no the other night. She had not been teasing; it had been a totally justifiable virginal fear of the unknown, which somehow made him feel a lot better, and yet worse at the same time. He had come on to her like a ton of bricks because he'd thought she was an experienced woman, and nothing could have been further from the truth.

Sally lay against Zac's chest and listened to his rapid heartbeat beneath her cheek. She heard his question, felt his hand on her head, but didn't look up. She couldn't…she was still throbbing internally in the aftermath of the most amazing experience of her life. Her body felt heavy, but paradoxically she was light-headed with the wonder at what had happened.

Never in her wildest dreams had she imagined sex to be so all-consuming—an intensely erotic ride on a one-way ticket to the stars. Zac wasn't just a magnificent lover, he was the absolute perfect lover, she was sure. But as the tremors finally subsided, and she relaxed into a lazy lethargy with his great body beneath her and the musky scent of sex all around them, she slowly began to recall her own eager, almost brazen actions, and she was embarrassed by them.

'Sally?' He tugged lightly on her hair. 'I asked you if you are okay.'

She had to face him some time, and, pressing her hands against his chest, she slipped down to lie at his side, casting him a sidelong glance. 'I'm fine,' she murmured, feeling inexplicably shy.

Zac rolled off the bed. 'I need the bathroom,' he grated.

'In the hall, opposite the kitchen,' Sally murmured, but he was already striding across the room, totally at ease with his naked state. Sally watched his progress, secretly admiring his tight bum and broad back. Tall, lithe and golden, he moved like a sleek jungle cat—all hard-packed muscle and sinew, with not a trace of fat on his massive frame. He was her lover, and a delicious little shiver stirred her sated body.

He had worn a condom—hence the bathroom,

she suddenly realised. Good, she told herself, but the unbidden thought entered her head, that while she had been lost in mindless ecstasy Zac had still had all his wits about him, and had taken no chances with his bachelor state.

Zac stood in the bathroom, his hands clasping either side of the basin, his head bowed. The best sex of his life, and he had been damned with *'fine'*. Not wonderful, not awesome, not even good. No, he'd got *fine*. On top of which he felt slightly ashamed—not an emotion he usually suffered from—because he had given her no choice but to sleep with him.

Sally had the ability to confuse and confound him like no other woman he had known, and for the first time in his adult life he actually doubted his sexual prowess. But only for a second.

He lifted his head and ran his hands through his hair. Sally had been with him all the way. She could not have faked her response. She had been like a living flame in his arms. It was her first time, so perhaps she was simply lost for words? And he should not have left her so abruptly—in his experience women liked to be cuddled after sex.

Having analysed her reaction to his own satisfaction, he dismissed the niggling doubt he felt and left the bathroom.

He stopped by the bed and looked down at her.

Her glorious red hair was spread across a pillow in a tangled mass of curls, her lips were swollen from his kisses, her exquisite body was spread across the white sheet in lax abandon, and instantly he began to harden again.

She glanced up at him. 'You're back,' she murmured, and moved to give him space. And then he saw the stain. He paused for a moment, then stretched out by her side. He swept a few strands of hair from her face, his expression sombre.

'You are sure I didn't hurt you?'

The touch of Zac's hand on her head and the warmth of his body reached out to Sally, and she lifted her eyes to his. For a moment she could have sworn she saw a look of uncertainty in the liquid depths.

'I am fine, honestly.'

'Damn it, Sally!' He scowled 'Do you have to say *fine* to everything?'

'What do you want me to say?' she asked teasingly. 'You were a magnificent lover and I only wish I had known what I was missing, then I would not have waited so long?' She tried a smile, ridiculously pleased he was back in bed with her.

'You should have told me you were a virgin.'

Zac actually sounded aggrieved, and out of nowhere Sally was reminded of all the countless times her mother had tried to appease her father in the past—anything to keep him longer at her side. And she was in danger of doing the same.

Suddenly an icy touch of reality pierced the mindless sexual cocoon that Zac had woven around her.

How like a man to make out it was the woman's fault... Then she remembered why she was there.

'What difference would it have made?' she demanded, and sat up, crossing her arms over her chest. If the coverlet had been anywhere to be seen she would have wrapped herself in it. She was here at Zac's command, because of what her father had done, and she would not forget again.

'Basically, you are paying my father for me to be your mistress.' She shot him a cold, derisory glance. 'I did try to warn you I might be bad at the job. So don't blame me if you got less than you bargained for.'

His ruggedly attractive face darkened with anger, his lips drawing back from his teeth. 'You're right,' he said tightly. 'It makes no difference at all.' His hand snaked out and caught a handful of her hair. 'As for being bad...you are a very bright lady and you will soon learn everything you need to know to please me.'

Their eyes met, and she gasped at the predatory look she saw in his, but it was not fear she felt but an atavistic desire.

He jerked her head down and her heart beat out of control as his mouth took hers in a fierce, possessive kiss. His hands dropped to her waist and he lifted her to straddle his thighs—and what followed was like nothing that had gone before…

She fell forward and put her hands out, either side of him, to stop herself ending up splayed against his chest. Her hair falling around her shoulders, she looked at him through her lashes, seeing the barely controlled hunger in his eyes.

'Stay like that.' The command was harsh, guttural, and, raising his head, he licked each pouting nipple with devastating effect. Fierce arrows of pleasure shot from her breast to her pelvis. She felt his hands running up and down her spine, his great body pressing up into her. She was amazed that he could arouse her so instantly after what they had just shared. Dropping her head, she brushed her lush, swollen lips against his and kissed him, her tongue exploring his mouth with a feverish delight that he immediately reciprocated. Suddenly he grasped her hair and pulled her head back.

'No more,' he rasped, his black eyes searing into her.

His strong hands lifted her hips and she felt the power of his erection pulsing between her thighs.

'I want to watch you—see the passion in your incredible eyes as you come for me.'

Sally closed her eyes to block out his dark, compelling gaze, a low moan escaping her as he positioned her to accept him. Her head fell back as he thrust up into her, the white-hot flames of passion growing as he lifted her, twisted her, bucked beneath her, driving her wild with the force of her need. She was oblivious to everything but his scent, his power, and the achingly exquisite pleasure, and she cried out as she shuddered helplessly, her body convulsing around him.

Still he did not stop. He reared up and without breaking contact placed her legs either side of his thighs. His hands flattened against her back, so her breasts were crushed against the hardness of his chest, and he took her mouth in deep marauding kiss that incredibly drove her higher again.

He demanded and she gave, their bodies locked together in a mutual, desperate, primitive mating. They kissed, they clawed, and finally he spun her beneath him. He paused and held her once again on the edge of ecstasy, his face a taut, dark mask of rigid control, his black eyes burning into hers.

'Please…' She groaned his name. 'Zac…'

'At last,' he growled, and thrust deeper and faster, until the fire of passion finally burned out of control, consuming them both.

For a long time the only sound in the stillness of the room was Zac's rasping breath. He lay with his head over her shoulder, his weight pinning her to the bed. Later Sally would hate him, and probably herself, but right now she hadn't the strength.

'Sorry…' he murmured, and rolled off her to lie at her side. 'I'm too heavy for you.'

And she had the oddest notion that the latter comment had been added as an afterthought. His *sorry* had been an apology for what had just exploded between them.

She didn't bother answering. She had been exhausted before Zac arrived, and now she was exhausted in a different and amazing way, her body sated and at rest. She didn't think she could even lift her head. Her heavy lids drifted over her eyes. All she wanted was sleep. She felt an arm reach around her shoulder and her eyes flew open.

'Sally, are—?'

She cut in. 'If you are going to ask me if I am okay, don't bother. I'm fine.'

But she was shocked and, yes, slightly ashamed. She didn't recognise the totally uninhibited woman she had become in response to Zac's expert lovemaking.

'You fulfilled your promise to be great in bed more than I could have possibly imagined,' she told him truthfully. After all, she had almost begged him at the last…his apologies were not necessary.

'But I really am too tired for any more tonight, so take your arm off me—you're wasting your time.'

His arm was withdrawn, and she felt strangely bereft.

'I was only going to cuddle you. Most women, I believe, like that sort of thing.'

'Well, you should know—you have had plenty of experience. Thanks, but no thanks.' She forced herself to look up at him; he was watching her, a dark, brooding expression on his hard face. 'All I want to do is sleep, so if you wouldn't mind leaving now…'

'I could run a bath for you. It will help you relax.'

'If I was any more relaxed I'd be unconscious. Please, Zac, just go. It must be late, and I have to be up for work in the morning.'

He slid off the bed and stood looking down at her. 'If you are sure I can't do anything for you?'

He'd done more than enough, Sally thought, but didn't say it. 'No—except close the door on your way out.' And she closed her eyes to block him from her view, because he actually looked and sounded as if he cared, which she knew he did not.

She listened to the muffled sounds of him dressing. She felt him place the coverlet gently over her and brush his lips against her cheek, and heard his murmured, 'Sleep well, Sally, and I'll see you tomorrow.' She didn't open her eyes. 'We have a deal, remember?'

She heard his footsteps on the wooden floor, and the door closing.

When she was sure Zac was gone Sally opened her eyes and slipped out of bed to pad along to the bathroom. She turned on the shower and stood under the soothing spray—except it did not soothe her. The events of the evening played over and over in her tired mind.

Zac and his ultimatum: become his mistress or watch her father destroyed. The amazing experience of making love—no, not love but lust. And Zac's reminder when he left that *they had a deal*.

All that and the actual reality of her life combined together to almost defeat her.

Overcome by a complex mixture of emotions, she felt the tears leak from her eyes. She cried for her mum and for herself until she had no tears left. Finally she turned off the shower, dried her eyes and her body, and walked back to bed. She withdrew a clean sheet from a cupboard in the unit, and changed the bedlinen. Then she took a cotton nightdress from a drawer, slipped it over her head and crawled into bed. She curled up into a ball and fell into a deep, blessedly dreamless sleep of sheer exhaustion.

CHAPTER NINE

SALLY blinked and opened her eyes. The brilliant rays of the morning sun shining through the window had woken her. Good, the rain from last night had stopped and the sky was a perfect blue, she noted, and stretched her limbs prior to getting out of bed. Then she remembered, as muscles she had not known she had screamed in protest.

She closed her eyes again, in a futile attempt to block out what had happened. But it was no good. A vivid image of Zac's naked body poised over hers flashed in her mind: the moment he'd possessed her, and her own avid response not once but again and again. Her nipples tightened at the memory. She had almost begged him to take her the last time... Ashamed at her own reaction, she leapt out of bed and dashed to the bathroom.

Showered and dressed in a green button-through shirt-style dress in easy-care cotton, bought from a High Street department store, she made and drank a cup of coffee and ate a bowl of cornflakes. She washed the china in the sink and stood it on the draining board. Then, taking her keys off the hook on the wall, she put them in her taupe leather shoulder bag. She slipped her feet into flat matching sandals and, flinging the chain strap of her bag over her shoulder, she headed for the door.

The ringing of the telephone stopped her in her tracks. Her heart sank. Please not my mother, she prayed, and answered the phone.

'Good morning, Sally,' a deep husky voice drawled in her ear, setting every nerve in her body on edge. Oh, no! she groaned silently. Zac.

'Good morning,' she said stiffly. 'What do you want? And make it fast—I am on my way to work.'

'You know what I want, Sally. You,' he delivered, with a deep throaty chuckle. 'But for now I will settle for knowing what time you finish work. I will pick you up.'

'That isn't necessary,' she snapped, and was glad he could not see her blush. 'I will be back here by seven-thirty at the latest.'

'Not good enough… What time, Sally?' he demanded, all humour banished from his tone.

Reluctantly she told him five-thirty, and hung up.

Zac had done his homework and discovered that the museum staff usually left by a side exit door with a short flight of steps leading down to the pavement. He parked the black Bentley Coupe on the opposite side of the road and checked the time: five minutes to go. Leaping out, he leant casually against the passenger side of the car, his legs crossed at the ankles, and waited. He was totally unaware of the admiring glances cast his way by the passing female population, his whole attention focused on the exit.

He saw Sally the moment she walked out of the door, and he swept his gaze leisurely over her even as his groin tightened in instant response at the sight of her. She was wearing a simple jade-green dress, and the evening sun glinted gold on her red hair, looped in a knot of curls on top of her head. She was a vision in green and gold and she was all his… But not tonight. He was determined to keep his libido in check.

Sally was new to sex and she needed time to recover and to come to terms with what had happened between them. He had not been the most sensitive of lovers, certainly not the second time, and though the sex had been incredible he wasn't exactly proud of the fact.

The beginnings of a smile curled his lips but quickly turned to a frown as he realised she was not alone. A tall, blond-haired man, impeccably dressed and carrying a briefcase, was at her side.

Sally stopped on the bottom step, and the man said something to her that made her laugh. He flicked a stray curl from her face and kissed her cheek, then turned and strolled away with a wave.

Sally waved goodbye to her boss and turned to step down onto the pavement. She glanced to left and right. With a bit of luck Zac would be waiting at the front of the building and she could avoid him a little longer, she thought, still smiling. Then she glanced across the road and her heart missed a beat.

Zac was leaning with negligent ease against the side of a black convertible. Tall, his olive-toned skin sun-kissed to a deep gold, his black hair dishevelled, he was wearing navy trousers and a pale blue shirt, with a cashmere sweater draped across his broad shoulders.

How was it, she wondered, that Italian men had a way with casual clothes like no other nationality? He looked every inch the Italian tycoon, and pure alpha male. He made no move to approach her, but simply lifted a hand in greeting…or was it a command? Either way, it made no difference. Her choice had been made last night, and she walked across the road and stopped in front of him.

'Hello…' Lifting her chin, she connected with his dark eyes and said inanely, 'I see you found me okay.' Suddenly she was having difficulty breathing as his virile sexuality hit her like a blow to the heart. Not twenty-four hours ago she had been naked in bed with this man, behaving in a previously unimaginable way. Her cheeks turned pink at the thought.

'Did you doubt it?' he asked, with an arrogant arch of one ebony brow.

'No, no…' she murmured, taking a step back just as a car whizzed past.

Two strong hands grasped her waist and swung her high off the ground, dropping her into the passenger seat of the convertible. 'Sit down before you get knocked down,' he said, and, crossing to the driver's side, he slid in beside her. He made no effort to start the car.

He turned to look at her, one hand on the steering wheel, the other arm draped along the back of the soft leather seat.

'So who is the blond guy?'

Sally frowned, thoroughly flustered and not sure what he was talking about. No hello, no kiss… Not that she wanted one, of course… Just a snapped question.

'I asked who was the man that kissed you goodbye.'

'Oh, you mean Charles—my boss.'

'I might have guessed. A kind, caring boss, I

seem to recall you telling me. Now I know why. He wants you for himself.'

'Don't be ridiculous. He is a thoroughly decent man, and friendly with all his staff.'

'I bet he does not kiss them all,' he drawled derisively. '*Dio*, Sally, you can't be that naïve.' He shook his dark head. 'He is a man, and you are a very beautiful woman he sees every day at work. You must know he lusts after you.'

'You are totally wrong—he is a happily married man with a child.' For an instant Sally wondered if Zac was jealous…

'As is your father, and according to you it never stopped *him*.'

'That is a horrible thing to say—but coming from you it does not surprise me.'

He wasn't jealous. He was simply being his usual arrogant self, presuming every man's motives were as basic as his own.

'Charles is a happy, totally committed married man, proud of his family—and I know because I have met his wife and daughter on countless occasions. So drop this pointless conversation and drive on. You're blocking the traffic,' she snapped, oddly dispirited by his attitude.

Zac was not convinced. He knew his fellow men. Married or single, few if any would be unaware of a woman as exquisite as Sally. Even Raffe, his assistant, happily married for five years, had taken one look at her, his eyes lighting up, and declared her gorgeous.

He started the car and smoothly pulled out into the rush-hour traffic. He glanced sidelong at Sally and saw again the sadness in her expression. He could have kicked himself for being such a callous idiot.

The first time they had met he had been irritated by the way she had virtually ignored him, but now he realised that, thanks to her father's ill-conceived behaviour and her mother's illness, she unconsciously dismissed any man who showed an interest in her. If last night had taught him anything it was that Sally truly was an innocent, and naïve when it came to men—hardly surprising, given she worked for a living and spent most of her free time visiting her mother.

The silence between them stretched and stretched, and even with bustle of the city all around them Sally was beginning to get nervous. 'Where are we going?' she finally asked, as the car stopped at some traffic lights.

'I know a nice restaurant on the south coast overlooking the sea, about an hour's drive from here.'

'We are going out?'

Somehow she'd thought he would take her straight back to her apartment, but obviously not. So he could not be in that much of a hurry to get her back into bed.

'Good,' Sally murmured, and squashed the little devil voice in her brain that suggested otherwise.

'Unless, of course, you had something else in mind? I'm easy…' Zac drawled, giving her a lazy, sensuous smile that made her all too aware of what he was suggesting.

'No, the seaside sounds great. I used to live by the sea until I moved to London to work. And after mum's accident the house in Bournemouth was sold.' She frowned. 'Actually, when I think about it I have not been to the beach in over a year.'

They ate dinner on the terrace of a restaurant perched on a hilltop, overlooking a small cove where a few fishermen's cottages surrounded the beach.

Sally chose pâté as a starter, as did Zac, and he ordered lobster with salad for the main course, followed by summer pudding and coffee.

They shared a bottle of wine, and Zac quizzed her about her childhood and her days as a student. She did the same, and discovered his parents had actually died when he was one. Far from being born with a silver spoon in his mouth, as she had thought, she was amazed when he told her he had spent his early years in an orphanage and worked for every single cent he had made. Some of his stories were funny, like the one about his abortive attempt to make his own olive oil, and how he had finally called in an expert. He made her laugh, and for once she allowed herself to relax.

'More wine?' Zac asked, holding the bottle over her glass. His dark eyes, still lit with amusement, were holding hers.

'Fine.' She smiled, and he filled her glass without comment. She picked it up and took a sip.

Then Sally saw him grimace, and the humour faded from his dark eyes. Perhaps he thought she was drinking too much. It struck her that he had only had one glass all through the meal and this was her third.

'Perhaps not,' she murmured, about to replace her glass on the table.

'Yes, drink, Sally—enjoy it. It is an excellent wine, but when I am driving I only allow myself one glass with a meal.'

Enjoying the relaxed ambience of the evening gave her the confidence to ask him boldly, 'So why the grimace?'

'It is that word *fine*. When we first met I noticed you use it an awful lot when you are not bothered either way. Even last night, after we had incredible sex, you used it again. Why?'

'Oh…' She suddenly remembered him returning from the bathroom last night and sliding into bed beside her, asking her the same question. She hadn't answered him then, but now, fuelled by more wine than she was used to, she thought, why not?

'I had a terrible stutter as a child, and it is a habit I developed because for some reason I could almost always say *fine* without a problem. I quickly realised it was a very versatile word. Fine with a smile was a yes; fine with a shrug was no. It could mean good or great or simply okay. My father used to laugh when I began to stutter, but my mother took me to a speech therapist and I was eventually cured. The habit lingers.'

Zac was shocked, and disgusted with himself. Sally had faced a huge problem as a child and beaten it, while he had behaved like a complete idiot by allowing one word to bother him. 'I'm sorry, Sally. It must have been hard for you, and it was crass of me to ask. Forgive me.'

Sally had registered the expression of disgust on Zac's face and she wasn't surprised. A supreme male like Zac expected perfection in his women, and now she had told him her secret he was obviously disappointed.

'Of course. Forget about it,' she said with a brief smile, and, turning, she looked out into the distance. The sun was slowly sinking towards the distant horizon, turning the sky to a palate of pale blue, pink, red and gold, and she had a feeling Zac's interest in her would sink just as quickly now he'd realised she wasn't quite the perfect woman he had imagined.

'How on earth did you find this restaurant?' she asked, in a deliberate change of subject, but nevertheless enchanted by the vista before her. Turning back to look at him, she added, 'I've never heard of the place, never mind the restaurant.'

'I like to drive, and I discovered it one day when I got lost,' Zac admitted with a rueful grin.

'You? Lost? That does surprise me—but I am glad you were,' she quipped. 'June is my favourite month, with the long light nights, and this view is absolutely spectacular.' Her blue eyes swept along the coastline and back out to the sea, as smooth as the proverbial millpond and reflecting the sun's rays in a band of gold.

'The view *is* incredibly beautiful,' Zac agreed, and she glanced back to find he was not looking at the view but at her, and the expression in the depths of the dark eyes that met hers sent a rush of heat careering through her slender frame.

'Yes, and the food is good as well.' She glanced down at her plate, battling to fight back the blush that threatened. It was to no avail. Her cheeks were turning a delicate shade of pink.

'There is no need to be embarrassed because you want me, Sally,' Zac drawled throatily, a hint of satisfaction in his tone 'It is perfectly natural, and you must know after last night how desperately I want you. If I had my way I would keep you with me all the time, for as long as this passion, this hunger between us, lasts.'

The deep, dark, slightly accented drawl sent shivers down her spine, and her pink cheeks turned to a scarlet to rival the setting sun as she imagined spending all her time with Zac, sharing his bed and his life. Then she fell back to earth with a thud. For a second she had been in danger of forgetting why she was there.

'That's not possible…'

'I know—you have your mother and your work.' He reached over the table and clasped one of her slender hands in his. 'I can appreciate your mother is deserving of your time, but I am not so happy about your work since seeing your boss.'

'Not that again.' She tried to pull her hand free, but he tightened his grip.

'So long as you understand, Sally, that in a relationship I demand total exclusivity from the woman I am with and give it in return.'

'When would I have the time, even if I had the inclination?' she asked derisively.

He looked at her for a long, silent moment, and then he stood up and pulled her to her feet and into his arms. 'You have a smart mouth, Sally, and I know just the way to close it,' he said quietly, and, dipping his head, he kissed her. She collapsed against him like the proverbial pack of cards.

When he finally let her go her face was flaming with embarrassment and her eyes were dark with arousal. She couldn't begin to imagine what the other customers thought of this public display.

'That was…' she began.

'Successful. It silenced you,' he said, and after paying the bill he took her hand in his and led her out of the restaurant towards the parked car.

The evening air was a blessing to Sally's over-heated skin, and she stopped and took a deep, calming breath, reluctant to get in the car. She glanced around, anywhere but at Zac, and was struck again by the beauty of the place.

'Do we have to leave straight away?' she asked. 'I have been cooped up in the basement of the museum all day, and I'd like to walk along the beach for a while.'

'Sure,' he agreed, threading his fingers through hers, and they walked down the steep hill to the small cove.

The sun was a blazing circle of gold as it slowly dipped to the horizon, and the moon was already showing in the sky over the opposite cliff, creating a magical natural picture that no artist, however brilliant, could ever aspire to.

A slight breeze from the sea made her shiver slightly, and Zac, without saying a word, took his sweater and knotted it around her shoulders.

'No, you keep it.' She tried to object. 'You are accustomed to a much hotter climate—you need it more than me.'

He laughed—a low, husky sound. 'Sally, your concern is touching but not necessary.' He placed an arm around her shoulders so she could not remove the sweater. 'I am not likely feel a chill with you by my side.' His eyes slid to hers, narrowed and unreadable. 'Here or anywhere.'

Sally stared at him for a moment, trying to read the expression on his face and failing. Then she turned her head and watched the sea, evading his eyes.

'I suppose, compared to Italy and the other places you have been, this does not look that spectacular.'

'Trust me, this is spectacular,' Zac drawled as they walked down towards the waterline and stopped just out of reach of the gently lapping waves. 'But you're right. The view of the sea and the southern Italian coastline from my home in Calabria is very beautiful.'

'Is that where you live?'

'I have a house in that area, yes, though I spend most of my time at my apartment in Rome, as the head office of my company is based there,' he told her as they strolled along the beach. 'At the moment I am staying in my apartment in London.'

'You actually have an apartment in London?'

she asked, her curiosity aroused; she had thought he would be staying in some top-class hotel.

'Yes. I keep an apartment in a block I own there. I tend to do that in most of the multi-occupancy properties I buy. I have others in New York, Sydney and South America. I have decided there is a better return on apartment blocks than hotels; they take less organising, much fewer staff and a fraction of the running costs.'

'Nice…' she murmured. He sounded like the tycoon he was, and she would do well to remember that. He was an incredibly wealthy, sexy man. Not for him an assignation with his latest lady in a hotel, when he had apartments all over the world.

'I'll show you the apartment tomorrow night, if you like.'

'Fine,' she said, and stopped. 'Sorry—it just slipped out.'

'No need to apologise—now I know the reason behind your habit I think it is rather endearing.' He grinned and, pulling her close, smoothed her hair back from her face and brushed her lips with his. She shivered.

'You are cold. We are leaving,' he said, for once totally misreading her reaction—for which she was grateful.

Zac got to her with an ease that amazed her and also made her afraid. Sex was one thing, she told herself, but she didn't want to feel anything else for him. Yet it was becoming more and more difficult—especially after this evening, when he had revealed his upbringing to her.

'Sally?' She heard the deep-toned voice and slowly opened her eyes. 'We are back.'

'Oh…' She had fallen asleep, with her head resting on Zac's arm and her hand on his thigh. 'Sorry—I didn't mean to sleep,' she said, her fingers flexing on his thigh as she straightened up.

A wry smile twisted his firm lips. 'I rather enjoyed your hand stroking my thigh, but it did not do a lot for my driving skill,' he drawled in self-mockery.

'I didn't—did I?' she gasped.

He chuckled 'You will never know, Sally. Come on, you are tired. Let's get you to bed.'

And, stepping out of the car, he walked round the bonnet while Sally was trying to control her suddenly racing pulse. Was he coming to bed with her?

Zac opened the passenger door and held out a hand to her. She took it and stepped onto the pavement. She looked up into his darkly attractive face, lit by the street lamp. His expression was bland. He gave nothing away.

'Thank you for a nice evening,' she murmured politely as, fingers entwined, they walked into the foyer of her apartment block. Then, pulling her hand from his, she turned to face him. 'You do know you are illegally parked, Zac? Your car will get either ticketed or towed, so you don't need to come up with me,' she told him, trying to be assertive.

'Yes, I do need,' he drawled softly, and dipped his head and took her lips in a long, lingering kiss.

Zac had set out this evening full of good intentions to wine and dine Sally, like on a conventional date, then leave her with a kiss at her door. But as the evening had progressed his good intentions had begun to fade, and, having endured an hour-long drive with her snuggled up against him, he was having trouble remembering them at all.

'But what about your car?'

He put an arm around her shoulder and led her into the elevator. She looked up at him with big, wary eyes, but she could not disguise the awareness lurking in the smoky-blue depths.

Zac smiled at her genuine concern, and dropped a brief kiss on the top of her head. 'They can ticket it, tow it—do what they like with it. I…' He was going to say he could not do without her, but stopped. 'I insist on seeing you safely to your door,' he amended.

He had never actually needed a woman so badly that he could not do without her for a night, and it worried him. He had the troubling thought that it would take a whole lot longer to physically tire of Sally than any other woman he had ever met or was likely to.

The elevator doors opened and he paused for a moment. Maybe he should walk away now… Then he saw her standing in the hall, and she glanced over her shoulder at him, a question in her brilliant blue eyes. He put his hand on the elevator door to stop it closing and followed her.

'Give me your key.' He took it from her hand, opened the door to her apartment and ushered her inside. Before she said a word, he turned her into his arms and bent his dark head to taste her sweet, intoxicating mouth.

A long, breathless moment later, Sally stared up into Zac's dark eyes. 'Would you like a coffee?' she asked softly. Held close against him, the strength of his arousal pressing against her belly, she was achingly aware of what he wanted—and it wasn't coffee…

He smiled—a slow curl of his firm lips. 'No, I want to undress you.' And, reaching for the buttons of her dress, he began to unfasten them one by one.

Sally let him.

She told herself there was no point in resisting, but the reality was she didn't want to, as excitement fizzed in her veins like the finest champagne.

He reached her waist and unfastened the belt. Slipping his hands beneath the collar, he eased the dress down her arms to let it fall in a pool at her feet. He lowered his head and covered the pulse that beat madly in her throat, sucking gently.

'And then I want to put you to bed,' he murmured, his breath warm against her ear as he unfastened her bra and peeled it off, exposing her naked breasts to his intent gaze.

'That's better,' he said huskily, and, dipping his head, he licked each rosy peak before slipping his hands underneath the lace of her briefs and sliding them down to her hips.

A gasp of surprise escaped her as he knelt down in front of her and, lifting her feet one at a time, removed her sandals, before reaching once more for her briefs. Slowly he peeled the scrap of lace down her now trembling legs and repeated the procedure, finally removing them completely.

He looked up at her though the thick curl of his lashes. 'Exquisite…' he murmured, and before she knew what he intended his hands had grasped her waist. He kissed the flat plain of her stomach and lower, to nuzzle at the apex of her thighs.

'No!' She tried to pull back.

'You are right. You are not ready yet for what I had in mind.' Zac rose to his feet and, swinging her up in his arms, carried her to the bed. He pulled back the coverlet and laid her gently down, then pulled the cover back over her and straightened up.

She stared up at him, her luminous blue eyes reflecting her puzzlement. Surely he was going to join her? Then she remembered—he had said she was not ready…

'So I am not mistress material after all?' she murmured.

He did not answer, but looked down at her with a strange expression on his face, broodingly solemn. Then, taking his wallet from his pocket, he flipped it open and took out a card. 'These are the numbers you can contact me on any time. The last is my personal cell phone.' He dropped it on the bedside table.

'That isn't necessary. You know where to find me.' She did not fully understand what had happened from his stripping her naked to becoming the cool, aloof man before her.

'Let me be the judge of what is necessary.' And, bending over her, he kissed her slowly, tenderly. 'Go to sleep, Sally. I'll see myself out and see you tomorrow.'

The night air was cold, and Zac stopped on the pavement to put his sweater on before getting into his car. He started the engine, a tender smile curling his mouth as he thought of the look of puzzlement on Sally's face when he had tucked her up in bed. It had stretched his control to the limit to leave her instead of joining her. The image of stripping off her clothes and her standing naked in his hold flashed in his head. Not a good idea when he was driving, and he shifted uncomfortably in his seat.

He hadn't intended on having sex with Sally tonight, and strictly speaking he had not—the pain in his groin could testify to the fact. But he had not walked away as he'd intended. He hadn't been able to keep his hands off her.

A frown pleated his broad brow. He had realised when she'd murmured about not being mistress material that Sally really wasn't, and it bothered him. He wished that he had never made the distasteful deal with her, but dated her in a conventional way…

As for her guidelines… He shook his dark head. He had nothing to worry about; he was seeing her tomorrow night. She had agreed to have a look at his apartment, and once she saw it he knew her guidelines and hopefully their deal would be forgotten. The next time they had sex would be in a king-size bed, and he could hardly wait.

Sally lay where Zac had left her, her body aching with frustration, hardly able to believe he had walked out. She told herself she didn't care, that she was glad he was gone and had spared her another night of sex, but in her heart of hearts she knew she lied. Obviously to a worldly, sophisticated male like Zac she fell short of what he was used to in the bedroom stakes. She should be pleased if he had tired of her already. She knew he was a man of his word and would not renege on his deal with her father, but bizarrely the thought gave her no joy.

CHAPTER TEN

THE next evening Sally walked out of the museum and her heart leapt. Her blue eyes landed on Zac, who was standing on the bottom exit step. Immaculately dressed in a dark business suit and snowy-white shirt, he was the epitome of a sophisticated mega-tycoon, and Sally had trouble believing she had actually made love with the man. But the sudden rush of heat to her face reminded her all too swiftly.

He covered the steps between them in a few lithe strides.

'At last,' he murmured and, taking her head between his hands, he kissed her firmly on the mouth. 'You're late.'

Breathless, she stepped back—and bumped into Charles, who was following her out. His arm came round her waist to steady her.

Zac's hand caught her arm. 'Steady, *cara.*' He smiled, drawing her to his side. 'You might give the man the wrong impression.' And, glancing at an astonished-looking Charles, he continued, 'You must be Sally's boss—Charles. Sally has told me so much about you. Nice to meet you.' He held out his free hand.

Sally looked from one to the other in shocked disbelief as Charles automatically shook Zac's hand, his glance taking in the possessive arm now draped around her shoulders before he looked at her with a puzzled expression on his face.

'You are all right, Sally? You know this man?'

But before she could open her mouth Zac cut in.

'Oh, yes—she knows me intimately. Don't you, sweetheart?'

She blushed scarlet and wanted to kick him. Instead she turned to Charles. 'Zac Delucca, a recent acquaintance of mine,' she offered reluctantly.

'You English are so reserved. Acquaintance, indeed.' Zac, every inch the dominant male, gave her a blatantly sexy look before turning to Charles and adding, 'In my country we would say lover.'

'Here we would not be so blunt,' Charles responded, holding Zac's arrogant gaze. 'And it is really no concern of mine except that Sally is a valued member of my team and a dear friend. You'd better take care of her.' He glanced back at Sally and smiled. 'I hope your mother is okay, and I'll see you on Monday. Goodbye.' And with a nod of his head to Zac, he left.

Sally watched him go, and then she saw the big black limousine parked on the road directly outside the exit. It simply added to the anger she was feeling. Furious, she shook Zac's arm off her shoulders.

'What on earth are you playing at? You promised no one would know about us, and you turn up here like I don't know what.'

'Like an animal staking out his territory?' he offered helpfully, and laughed at her look of horror. 'What do you expect, Sally?' He took her elbow and urged her down the steps to the waiting limousine. The chauffeur held open the door and she got in. Zac slid in beside her and, grasping her chin, turned her head to face him.

'I only agreed to your parents being kept in ignorance of our relationship,' he said. 'While I guard my privacy, I refuse to treat our relationship as a sordid secret. As for your boss—I know he wants you, and I am a possessive man. I keep what is mine. I was simply warning him off. The straightforward approach is usually the best, I find. You should take it as a compliment,' he declared outrageously, and shot her a wicked teasing smile.

'You are unbelievable,' she murmured, shaking her head as the chauffeur manoeuvred the car through the rush-hour traffic.

'So I have been told,' he muttered, his attention distracted by the ringing of his phone.

She glanced at him, but he had taken the phone from his jacket pocket and his dark eyes were narrowed in concentration—but not on her.

'If you don't mind, I have a few calls to make—some business to settle.' And, not waiting for her answer, he began talking in rapidfire Italian to whoever was on the other end.

Zac made her head spin. She didn't understand a word he was saying, but his deep, melodious voice sounded even more seductive in his own language. Seated next to him, with the all-male scent of him teasing her nostrils, and her lips still tingling from his kiss, she was in danger of him taking her over completely. Possessive, he had said—which she supposed *was* a compliment in a way. At least he had not added *for as long as it lasts.*

The car stopped and she looked around. 'We are in an underground car park!' she exclaimed as the chauffeur opened the door and she stepped out.

'Brilliant observation, *cara*,' Zac remarked with a smile, suddenly appearing at her side and taking her hand in his. 'I promised to show you my apartment, remember?'

Sally caught the salacious, knowing male grin on the chauffeur's face as he stepped back. Zac might as well have said *come up and see my etchings*, she thought, totally embarrassed.

But fifteen minutes later, her embarrassment forgotten, she stood in the middle of a huge bedroom, one of three he had shown her in the penthouse, and stared in amazement at a double bed the size of small state.

A brown leather headboard ran along the top and curved a few feet around either side to incorporate what passed as bedside tables, she supposed. But they were nothing like anything she had ever seen before. A bewildering array of steel buttons and switches were inset into the leather, along with screens and flashing lights. It looked like the flight deck of a jumbo jet.

From what she had seen, the whole apartment was on a massive scale. The kitchen had looked like something out of space: high-tech and unfathomable to Sally's stunned gaze. The living area was all steel, glass and black leather, and the dining room looked out over a long terrace with a fantastic view down the Thames to the Houses of Parliament and beyond.

Suddenly two hands curved around her waist from behind and pulled her back against a hard male body, and she couldn't help drawing in a sharp breath.

'So what do you think of the place?' Zac asked, nuzzling her neck, his warm breath caressing her ear.

Pride said she should at least try to resist Zac, but he pulled her tighter and the rock-hard pressure of his erection against her bottom sent her pulse-rate into overdrive.

'It is very modern—the ultimate bachelor pad,' she managed to answer, and then Zac ran his tongue up the side of her neck and traced the whorls of her ear. It was impossible for Sally to hide the way her body was suddenly trembling and she gave up trying.

His hands stroked up to cup her breasts, his thumbs gently rubbing the tender tips through the soft cotton of the top she was wearing.

'Do you like it?' he asked, his lips warm against her throat, and she wasn't sure if he meant the apartment or what he was doing to her.

But Sally said yes anyway, as he turned her around and lifted her top clear over her head and dispensed with her bra.

'You take my breath away, Sally,' Zac said huskily, his smouldering gaze sweeping over her half-naked body in almost worshipful appreciation.

He lifted his hands to caress her breasts, his long fingers teasing the tender tips into tight, ultra-sensitive arousal. A whimper of delight escaped her, and he caught it with his mouth and kissed her with a deep erotic skill that totally beguiled her.

His hands dropped to her waist and deftly removed her skirt, but she didn't notice. The same dizzying excitement and anticipation sizzled through her veins as during the first time he touched her, but now it was so much more intense as she knew the pleasure that was to follow.

Zac swept her up in his arms and eased her briefs off her legs, placing her gently in the middle of the huge bed.

'I have waited almost two days for this, and it is killing me,' he groaned, his glittering black eyes sweeping over her naked body, displayed for his delectation on the taupe coverlet.

Sally watched as he shed his clothes with a minimum of effort, and marvelled anew at his broad hair-roughened chest, at the all-male power and beauty of his naked bronzed body. He came down beside her and stroked a hand over her breast to the junction of her slender thighs. Her body bucked in response as his seeking fingers found her moist and ready.

Her hands moved over his muscular chest to curve around his broad shoulders. Her whole body shook with excitement, and instinctively she squirmed against him and drew a teasing finger down the length of his spine.

A deep shudder racked his mighty frame, and, catching her hand, he rolled over her and caught her breathlessly parted lips in a fierce kiss. Then his head dipped and his mouth found the rigid tip of her breast, suckling with an urgent need that made her groan out loud. Nudging her legs apart, he slid between them.

Sally lost all sense of time and place as Zac swept her along on a vast wave of passion that finally left her sprawled over his chest, her body still pulsing in the aftermath of his hungry, driven possession.

'I needed that,' he rasped. 'It was incredible.' His hands stroked softly down her back to her thighs and back up, to thread through the tangled mass of her hair. '*You* are incredible, my Salmacis.'

'I warned you—I do not answer to my given name,' she murmured softly, then did the opposite. 'You have no idea how embarrassing it can be when I'm introduced to people and I have to explain what it means,' she told him, with a soft, languorous smile curving her mouth. She was floating on a sea of pleasure, and she was too happy to argue.

'You answered me!' he quipped. 'But I understand it might be a problem. I won't use it in public, but I think of you as Salmacis when we make love, and by that point my first priority is rarely getting an explanation from you.' He chuckled.

'You are incorrigible.' She grinned, her blue eyes lingering on his darkly attractive face. How had she ever thought he wasn't handsome? Zac was utterly gorgeous.

'Maybe, but right now I am insatiable.' And he

proceeded to arouse her all over again, with a slow, skilful intimate exploration of her shapely body.

When his long fingers parted her thighs and found her hot and wet he rasped, 'And so, it seems, are you.'

She gave a long, shuddering groan as her body vibrated in fierce delight at the subtle stroke of his fingertips against her intimate quivering flesh. Her back arched as he moved down her body, lingering to suckle each breast before dipping his dark head lower still. His sinfully sexy mouth delivered the ultimate intimacy, the flick of his tongue teasing and tasting the tiny nub of feminine pleasure to pulsing arousal. He suddenly stopped. With every sensitised nerve screaming out for release she reached for him involuntarily, her slender fingers grasping at the black silken hair of his head.

He looked up through his thick curling lashes and murmured, 'Now you are ready for this, my sweet Salmacis.'

What followed drove her completely out of her mind as her body tensed to breaking point and she tumbled over the edge into a tumultuous release.

'What about you?' she murmured, when she was finally able to breathe again. The thick, rock-hard length of him was pressing against her still quivering stomach. 'You didn't…'

'Oh, I will.'

He covered her mouth with his own, and just

when she thought she had no more to give Zac proved her wrong. Slowly he began to kiss and caress her in a deeply erotic exploration of her body, his mouth returning to her breasts to suckle on their hard, throbbing peaks.

Her whole body was suffused with sensual heat, and she quaked with need. The intensity of the pleasure he gave her was almost pain. She clung to him, her nails scoring his back as he lifted her hips and thrust into her with long, deep strokes, stretching, filling her with a power and passion that drove her once more to the pinnacle of ecstasy and held her there.

She cried out, 'Please, please, Zac—now.' Her inner muscles clenched around his throbbing hardness as he plunged deeper into her eager body and carried them both to a ferociously orgasmic climax.

Sally lay across his chest, her body sated and her breathing slowly returning to normal. How long she lay there, listening to the heavy beating of his heart gradually subside, she had no idea. Finally she raised her head and looked lovingly down at Zac's bronzed features. His heavy-lidded eyes were closed, his long black lashes curling on his high cheekbones, and somehow he looked younger, not so hard, even a little vulnerable in his sleep.

She smiled to herself, relishing the pleasure it

gave her to study him in secret. She lifted a finger and tenderly stroked the line of his now shadowed jaw, and then up over his cheekbone to smooth the perfectly arched black brows. Her finger lingered on the small scar above one eyebrow and she wondered how he'd got it.

His eyes opened.

'I thought you were asleep,' she murmured.

'No, just savouring your touch. Carry on, my Salmacis.'

'How did you get this?' she asked. His huskily voiced request was oddly endearing, and the afterglow of making love encouraged her to be bold.

'In a fight when I was a teenager,' he murmured.

'That does not surprise me somehow—though I am surprised anyone managed to cut you.' She smiled, letting her gaze roam with feminine appreciation over the width of his shoulders and the muscular biceps of his strong arms. 'Who was it?' she asked.

'I can't remember his name now. I fought so many.'

Sally was intrigued. 'You mean you actually got into so many fights you can't remember what they were about? That is terrible.'

'No, I fought professionally until I was twenty. That is how I made the money to start my business empire.'

She looked at him with big, soulful eyes. He

truly was a remarkable man. He had actually fought physically to enable him get where he was today. How many punches, how much pain must his magnificent body have had to suffer as a teenager? The thought of anyone hurting him horrified her.

'Zac, you are amazing.'

'Thank you,' he responded with a rogue smile. 'You are pretty amazing yourself.' And he kissed her, then let his fingers run down the length of her hair. 'I love your hair.'

Sally's heart stopped for a second. She had actually thought he was going to say *I love you*, and her mellow mood was broken. How foolish was that? They had made love for hours and it had scrambled her brain, she swiftly told herself. She didn't *want* Zac to love her. She didn't believe in love. And yet she could not dislodge the fear that assailed her…

'Thank you,' she responded in kind, and hoped Zac had not noticed her brief hesitation. She shook her head to free his hand from her hair. 'Now, what has a girl got to do to get fed around here?' she asked, with an attempt at a smile. Conveniently her stomach rumbled.

'Okay, I can take a hint.' Zac lifted her by the waist and laid her down on the bed. 'And you have already done it—quite spectacularly,' he told her with a devilish smile. 'What would you like to eat? Meat? Fish? Game? Name it and it is yours.'

'Fish—but can you actually cook?'

'Yes,' he said, turning to sit on the edge of the bed, his back to her. 'But I have no intention of doing so.'

And a moment later he was ordering a meal over the telephone—conveniently part of the stupendous headboard.

'We have forty minutes before the food arrives,' he told her, replacing the phone. 'Enough time to share a shower.' And he plucked her off the bed and carried her into the bathroom.

A lot later Sally, with her hair wringing wet, a broad smile on her face and the sound of Zac's laughter ringing in her ears, collapsed into a plastic cushioned chair that looked like something out of the fifties, a towel wrapped around her body.

Zac had slipped on jeans and a top and gone to collect the food when it arrived. Sally, on the other hand, barely had the strength to move. The man actually was insatiable, she decided...and she would not have him any other way. She loved every minute spent with him in bed—or anywhere else, for that matter.

She now freely acknowledged the disappointment she had felt and tried to deny last night, when he had left her naked and alone in bed. But he had certainly more than made up for it this evening. Not only great sex, but she felt she understood him better since he had told her about his fighting career. No wonder he appeared hard sometimes, when he had had to physically fight to survive as a teenager.

Then again, maybe it was because sex was new to her that she enjoyed it so much. she tried to reason with herself. But she knew in her innermost being it had everything to do with the man himself. She could not imagine sharing such intimacies with any man but Zac.

The huge shower, with its jets shooting out all over, had been a novel place to make love, she thought, a dreamy, reminiscent smile on her face. Zac had soaped her all over, kissed and caressed her, and she had returned the favour. She had stroked and soaped every part of his magnificent body and then, dropping to her knees, she had done what she had been longing to do but never had the confidence before.

She had let her slender fingers examine every inch of his thickened length in minute detail, in awe of the source of so much pleasure. She had felt him tense when her tongue had swept out to taste the velvet tip, and heard him groan as she'd continued further.

'No more,' he had finally grated, and, reaching under her arms, he had jerked her high in the air and thrust up into her in an explosion of need. She was convinced only a man of Zac's strength and vigour could possibly have supported her, locked to his great body, as he had driven them both to yet another mind-blowing orgasm.

Against all the odds, her own innate honesty was forcing her to admit she was halfway to falling in love with him, and strangely she was no longer so afraid—it did not worry her at all.

Carpe diem—live for the moment. That was her new motto, she decided. And there was no guarantee in life as to how many moments one had left…

With a carefree grin she got to her feet and, picking up the conveniently wall-mounted hairdryer at one side of the first of the twin white porcelain basins, she began methodically to dry her hair, running her fingers through it over and over again.

She looked at her refection in the mirrored door of the cabinet that stretched the length of the wall. Her face was flushed, her lips were swollen, and Zac's roughened jaw had left a few telltale marks. She looked what she was: a thoroughly loved-up woman, but a bit of a mess. Maybe Zac had a brush she could borrow, to try and style her wayward mass of hair into some kind of order? She could impress him with her smooth, elegant locks…

She pushed at the cabinet and a door in front of her sprang open. There was all the equipment one would expect to find in a man's bathroom, including a box of condoms, and, spying a brush, she picked it up. It was then she noticed there was also a half-used bottle of Dior perfume—definitely not male— a few black hairpins and a thick black elastic hairband.

Her carefree mood evaporated like smoke in the wind. It did not take a genius to work out that the last woman to share his bed and bathroom had been Margot, the raven-haired model from Tuesday night. Sally stumbled back in shock. Just the thought of Zac sharing with Margot the same intimacies he had shared with her was enough to make her feel sick to her stomach.

She sank back onto the plastic chair and drew in a choked breath as pain pierced like a knife in her heart. Her head fell forward, her hair forgotten as she blinked back the bitter tears that threatened. Despairingly she realised that, against her long-held belief in her immunity to love, she had done the previously unthinkable and fallen in love with the man.

No… It wasn't possible, her brain told her, but her heart didn't want to listen… Conflicting thoughts were tearing her apart. She had only known Zac a week, been intimate with him for only three days. It could not be love… She would not, could not, accept such weakness.

All her life she had watched her mother humour

her father every which way to try and keep his love, to keep him at her side. Well, Sally was made of sterner stuff. She took after her maternal grandma in character, and she was nobody's fool.

Sally had fallen in lust at the hands of an expert—as many a woman had before—and to drive the lesson home she rose to her feet, straightened her shoulders and returned to the cabinet. She brushed her hair back from her face and fastened it in a ponytail with the black band left by Zac's last lover. A salutary reminder of what a naïve idiot she had been even to think of trying to impress a man who quite happily had sex with two women in the same week… No wonder he kept a whole box of condoms and never, even in the heat of passion, forgot to use one, she thought bitterly. As for loving such a man—never.

She returned to the bedroom and, gathering her scattered clothes from the floor and bed, swiftly put them on. Then, picking up her purse and slipping her feet into her sandals, she left the scene of her downfall without a second glance.

CHAPTER ELEVEN

ZAC turned as she entered the dining room. 'You have dressed. I thought you might simply grab a robe. Or at least I hoped,' he said, with a wickedly sensual smile.

'I never thought,' she murmured, and tried to smile when really she felt like cursing him to hell and back. Then, directing her attention to the dishes of food laid out on the dining table, along with two plates and glasses plus a bottle of wine in an ice bucket, she added, 'This smells delicious. I am ravenous.' Actually, the reverse was true—she had totally lost her appetite—but she was determined not to let Zac know.

Standing there, in jeans and a polo shirt, he was all arrogant male, and he would scent weakness a mile off, she knew.

'Dinner is served, my lady.' He gave her a sweeping bow and pulled out a chair for her, then waited until she'd sat down. With a flourish he opened the wine, which turned out to be champagne, and, filling her glass, gave a toast. 'To us—and long may we last!'

Reluctantly she sipped the sparkling vintage. 'To us,' she responded, and forced herself to smile again, when basically she felt like scratching his eyes out. But she could not afford to.

No matter how much she despised his morals, or lack of them, she still had to stick to their deal until Zac decided otherwise. Her mother's future happiness was at stake, short though that future might be.

Bitterly she wondered how he could almost have sex with her one night, make love to the willowy Margot the next, then have the audacity to demand Sally become his lover the following night. She wasn't jealous, she told herself, simply disgusted. For a brief space of time she had let herself become besotted by a man. Well, never again, she vowed silently...

The food looked great, but she had to make herself eat, and every morsel tasted like ash in her mouth. She refused the sweet, and his offer of more champagne, and watched him fill his glass again. Then she lifted her own to take a sip of the now flat liquid.

'I've been thinking, Sally.'

She raised her head and met his dark eyes across the table.

'We should renegotiate our arrangement and place it on a more intimate basis.'

She almost choked on the champagne. Was he crazy? She might be inexperienced, but she was pretty sure they could not possibly be more intimate than they already were.

'I know we made a deal, and you stated your guidelines, but I want to change them—for the benefit of both of us. I would like you to move in here.'

He sounded as if he was discussing some business deal in a boardroom, and she was too shocked to speak.

'You know the sex between us is incredible, but you have to admit, nice as your studio is, the bed is a little too small—especially for me.' He shrugged his broad shoulders. 'Whereas here we have plenty of space and you can enjoy every comfort money allows,' Zac offered. 'Plus, I am a very busy man. I had intended taking a few weeks' holiday, but a project I am involved in is not going as smoothly as I hoped and fixing it is going to involve quite a bit of travelling. I would feel much happier if I knew you were living here, where the security is superlative.'

Sally listened, her anger and bitterness festering as he continued.

'Think about it, Sally. All your financial needs taken care of. No more secondhand gowns, but the best money can buy.'

And then he had the nerve to slant a very male, satisfied smile her way—as if he was offering her the crown jewels when in fact he was suggesting she become his live-in lover in London. She could not help noticing he had not suggested taking her with him on his travels. He probably had other women living in his properties dotted all over the world.

Zac's arrogance was unbelievable, and his last comment had filled her with such fury that she bowed her head, so he would not see the anger blazing in her eyes.

She fought down the bile that rose in her throat and battled to control her rage. Hard to believe a short time ago she had been in danger of believing she might love him. Well, no more delusions—and no more negotiating with the vile man…

'Sally? What do you say?'

Slowly she lifted her head her and said, 'No.' Pushing back her chair, she stood up and very deliberately glanced at the thin gold watch on her wrist— a twenty-first birthday present from her mother.

'No explanation? Just no?'

Only then did Sally allow herself to look at him. The watch was a timely reminder of why she could not lose her temper with the lecherous bastard. 'Exactly. We made a deal, and I will stick by it. You said you were a man of your word, and I expect you to stand by that.'

Zac's eyes narrowed. 'Wait a minute—what just happened here?' he demanded, and she would have laughed at the look of confusion on his face if she hadn't been so angry and—yes, she admitted it—deeply hurt...

'We have just spent hours indulging in the most incredible sex, and *no* is your immediate reaction to my generous suggestion?' He finished his drink and rose to his feet to move in front of her, his hands on her shoulders, his black brows drawing together in a frown. 'I don't see your problem with the idea. You are joking, yes?' he prompted, his accent thickening.

'No, I am not joking,' she said curtly, finding his use of the word *generous* an insult too far. Zac believed he could buy anything and anyone—well, not her... She would stick to the letter of their deal, but no more, and with that in mind she added, 'It is almost midnight, and Saturday is my time, in case you had forgotten. I need to call a cab and go home.'

His eyes narrowed with tightly controlled anger. 'No need to call a cab. The limousine will take—'

She cut him off with a bitter laugh.

'No, thank you. I saw the salacious look your driver gave me when we arrived here,' she said scathingly. 'I certainly don't need a repeat performance to remind me. A cab will do fine.'

Zac stilled, his mind running riot. He was furious

at her hard-headed attitude, and he could not believe the passionate, eager lover he had held in his arms could change into the cold-eyed woman before him. He had actually imagined he felt a connection beyond the sexual with Sally—enough to confide in her the truth of his fighting past, something he had never done with any woman. Maybe that was his mistake!

He had never asked a woman to move in with him before—in fact, he had never spent more than a weekend with a woman in his life. One night, two at most, and he could count on one hand how rare an occurrence that was for him. Yet he had offered Sally more than any other woman and she had turned him down flat.

Or had she? he wondered cynically. Power and wealth attracted some women, and he had both and had learnt to recognise the type. He would be a fool if he didn't see through every hard-headed gold-digger that came along. He had put Sally in that category at first and changed his mind. Then he remembered she had said she wanted to marry—maybe she had not been teasing him, as he had thought... Was her refusal of his offer a trick to get him hungry enough for her to give her the ultimate offer: marriage? He didn't know...but he meant to find out...

Sally watched him as the silence lengthened,

and when Zac finally responded, she tensed as his fingers tightened on her shoulders.

'I think I understand why you refused to move in here.' He surveyed her with dark-eyed arrogance. 'You worry about what people will think if you live in my apartment, an outdated anxiety in this day and age. As for the driver—if you don't like him he will be replaced.'

'You amaze me, Zac!' Sally exclaimed. 'You don't care a damn about anyone but yourself—as long as you get what you want, to hell with the rest of us poor mortals.' She shook her head, her eyes hating him. 'You treat people like puppets to be moved at your bidding. Well, keep your driver and keep your apartment. I am not interested in either them or you.'

'You were happy enough in my bed earlier, and eager to do my bidding,' he declared with a sardonic smile. 'I only have to touch you and you will be again. But be warned—if your refusal of my offer is simply a ploy to get what the majority of females want—a wedding ring—you are wasting your time.'

Sally's cheeks burned, and she was filled with an incredulous anger as his words sank home. He could not have chosen a better way to insult her, yet again, and he had made her hate him more by reminding her of her weakness and implying she was after a marriage proposal.

'Oh, please!' she cried. 'Don't kid yourself. I would not marry you or any man in a million years. I am here only because of my father,' she said scathingly, and wanting to hurt him, wanting to dent his ego, his arrogant pride, she continued, 'You and he are two of a kind. He actually *told* me to be nice to you, and you have to wonder what kind of man pimps his own daughter to his boss…' She sneered. 'And what kind of boss takes advantage of the fact.'

'I am nothing like your father,' he snarled, his face darkening in fury. 'And you were with me from the moment we met. You practically melted the first time we kissed—the same as I did.'

Sally's mouth hardened into a bitter, hostile line. 'I made a *deal* with my father, to back him and be nice to you when you called. In return he will come with me this weekend to visit his wife, Pamela—my mother—something he never does more than once in a blue moon. Something I was hoping to persuade him to do over lunch the first day you and I met. And we both know that didn't work,' she drawled derisively.

'I had to bargain for the presence of my father at my mother's bedside because for some reason my mother loves the man, and misses him. Heaven knows why. And that was the first reason I agreed to your deal. The second was keeping my father out of prison—again to keep my mother happy. I asked you for time to raise the money, and hopefully with the damn man's help I'd pay you back, but you would not give me time. Well, now I am not wasting what is technically *my time* on you. I am leaving. I am picking my father up at nine in the morning to make sure he keeps his side of the bargain. As for you and I...' she drawled, her blue eyes reflecting her contempt. 'You know when and where I'm available, as agreed under the terms of our deal.'

Sally felt the tension in every bone in her body as Zac stared at her in a bitter, hostile silence, and it took every inch of will-power she could muster to hold on to her self-control. She avoided his eyes, but she could feel his gaze burning into her.

Suddenly his hands fell from her shoulders and she was free. Surprised, she glanced up at him. His face was suffused with anger, a thin white line circled his tight mouth, and his eyes rested coldly on her like chips of ice. And yet she could not look away, could not move. The continuing silence hung between them like a great black thunder cloud, and neither one seemed able to break it.

Then, as if a veil had fallen over his face, his expression changed to one of hard indifference. He turned and crossed the room, picked up the phone and called a cab.

'As you so succinctly pointed out, it is almost

Saturday,' he drawled as he sauntered back towards her.

Sally saw how close he was, and knew she should step back, but she refused to let him intimidate her.

'The cab will be here in five minutes,' he informed her, his hand reaching out to grasp her hair, sliding off the band constraining it, his long fingers tangling in the glossy red locks.

'You are an intelligent woman, Sally. But you have met your match with me,' he told her chillingly.

His dark head bent and his arm slid round her, pressing her against his long body while his hard mouth moved ruthlessly on hers. Her pulse leapt, and she fought an internal battle to resist the seductive power of his kiss, but his fingers bit into her waist and she lost... Helplessly she arched against him, her hands of their own volition curving over his broad shoulders and clinging in shaming response.

He raised his head, his dark eyes gleaming down at her. 'You see, my Salmacis,' he drawled mockingly, 'blame your father, make all the excuses you like, but you want me as much as I want you, and some day you might admit it. When you do, you have all my numbers—call me.'

Mortified by her easy capitulation to his kiss, Sally jerked free of him and glanced up with a bitterness that belied the longing in her eyes. 'That will never happen.' Then, to her relief, the intercom rang. The cab had arrived.

Zac walked her down to the street without saying a word until he handed her into the waiting cab.

'I am going to Italy tomorrow. Maybe we will meet again some time.' He shrugged 'Your choice.' And, turning, he went back inside without a backward glance.

Sally told herself she was glad it was over between them as the cab moved off, but she had to blink away the moisture hazing her eyes.

Zac Delucca was six feet five, and right at this moment he felt about two inches tall—not a pleasant feeling, he acknowledged as he strode across to the drinks cabinet and poured whisky into a crystal glass. He downed it in one. He was furious with Sally, but more so with himself. He was man enough to know without question that she wanted him on a sexual level, but that Sally dared class him with her father had shocked him.

He was forced to take a long, hard look at himself, and he didn't much like what he saw. When had he become such a cynical bastard about the opposite sex that he had mistaken an innocent, hard-working young woman for a teasing little gold-digger out for what she could get?

He had to accept he had behaved less than honourably in demanding Sally become his mistress. It had never entered his head to do anything so outrageous before, and he definitely never would again. But Sally had the ability to get under his skin like no other woman, and blinded by lust and— yes—jealousy he had acted on impulse and completely out of character.

Zac prided himself on his honesty and fair dealing, but his pride had taken one hell of a battering when Sally had declared with brutal frankness that as far as she was concerned her dad had tried to *pimp* his own daughter to save his neck, and that Zac was just as bad for taking advantage of the fact…

He had never once considered her feelings, other than in the sexual sense, and she responded with avid delight to what he could give her in bed. But the burden she'd had to bear with her mother and father that had led her into his bed had not bothered him at all.

One of the reasons she had agreed to be his mistress was so she could make a bargain with her despised father and get the man to go and visit his wife. How sad was that…?

It was true that Sally had asked for time so she could try and pay the debt, and he had refused. Something he had completely forgotten in his determination to bed her. All of which made him as despicable in her eyes as her father, and he couldn't really blame her... She deserved much better treatment from the man in her life than he had given her.

He had behaved abominably, and Zac knew that if Sally truly believed what she had told him, he had to let her go. His confidence and his pride in himself as a man would allow him to do no less.

He poured another whisky and tried to tell himself the world was full of beautiful women and he didn't need Sally. By the time he had downed half a bottle he was convinced!

Zac had known from the start she was going to be trouble. So far every time they had met they had ended up arguing at some point, and it was driving him crazy... He should have listened to what his head had been trying to tell him from the beginning and walked away.

A good businessman knew when to cut his losses. He was going back to Italy tomorrow and to hell with her. As for a woman, there was always Lisa on hold in Milan...

Sally opened the door of her apartment and stumbled inside. Zac had said he might see her some time, but she knew it was goodbye. It was what she wanted, an end to the affair that had been forced upon her, so why did she feel so hollow inside?

She had no answer and, stripping off her clothes,

she slid naked into bed and pulled the cover up around her neck.

Tomorrow she was visiting her mother—with her father. When she had first set eyes on Zac she had been a woman on a mission… Well, now the mission was accomplished, she told herself. But it was a hollow victory, and she felt numb inside—no joy, no tears, just emptiness.

The next morning, heavy-eyed, she staggered into the bathroom and into the shower. Immediately, the memory of Zac and the shower they had shared the night before flashed in her mind. Ruthlessly, she stamped on the erotic vision and focused on the female articles Zac's previous lover had left in his bathroom.

She had done the right thing in refusing his offer to move into his apartment. They had a deal, and if he didn't want to keep it that suited her just fine. But to her horror, by the time she stepped out of the shower, stupid tears were streaming down her face.

Five hours later, the smile on her mother's face as Sally walked into her room with her dad was enough to make all the heartache worthwhile.

Sally excused herself an hour later, saying she wanted to do some shopping in the nearby city of Exeter.

But actually she could not stand to listen any longer to her father's rant about how he had been moved sideways by his new boss. Now he had to do twice as much work for the same salary, and he had decided he was definitely retiring in twelve months, so he could see a lot more of his wife.

'Oh, Nigel, it must be so difficult for you,' Pamela had offered, her love and concern for the thieving devil shining in her eyes.

Sally had wanted to scream. It was lies—all lies. Her dad knew Pamela wasn't going to last more than a year, because the doctor had contacted him after informing Sally that her mother's heart wouldn't hold out much longer, but her mum lapped it all up, like a puppy dog devoted to its master, so instead she'd left.

By the time she returned her mum was on her own and her father had gone back to the hotel—or so he had told his wife. Sally did not see him again until breakfast the next morning. It was a silent meal, except for her father stating he wanted to leave for London directly after lunch. Sally had no intention of doing so, and as they were using her car he'd have no choice. But in that she was wrong. Five minutes after entering his wife's room, he had got her mum to agree it was best they left early...

If anything was guaranteed to confirm what Sally had always thought about love and marriage, it was seeing her mother, who was dying, comforting her father, who was lying through his teeth.

CHAPTER TWELVE

RETURNING to her hated apartment on Sunday evening, Sally tried to tell herself she was glad Zac had gone back to Italy before she got in too deep. But it did not stop her checking her messages in the vain hope he might have called. How pathetic was that? she thought miserably as she climbed into bed. But it did not stop her hoping deep inside that he might turn up Monday to Friday, as per their deal and that was even worse!

Honesty forced her to admit that, blinded by jealousy, she had driven Zac away with her hateful comments. But it was for the best... She didn't love him, could not love him, she told herself, and feverishly brushed away the tears that were determined to fall. So what if she stayed in a few evenings waiting for a call that never came, and cried herself to sleep a night or two? It was a whole lot better than a lifetime of heartache.

But as a week passed with no word from Zac it

became harder to dismiss him from her mind. Being alone in bed at night—the bed she had briefly shared with Zac—reminded her all too vividly of the pleasure and the passion of his exquisite lovemaking. When she did sleep invariably her dreams were haunted by his image, his touch, and she awoke hot and aching.

On Friday, two weeks to the day since Sally had last seen Zac her friend Jemma told her she looked pale and miserable and in need of cheering up. She suggested a night out—dinner and the cinema. Sally agreed, and actually managed to enjoy the film.

But the next day, when she arrived at the nursing home, the little bit of good the night out had done her was immediately cancelled as she was met by the doctor in charge of her mum's case.

He had been trying to ring her on her mobile phone for the past two hours, but Sally was in the habit of switching it off while driving so had never received his call.

Apparently her mother had suffered a massive heart attack and slipped into a coma. The staff had made her as comfortable as possible under the circumstances, and her husband had been informed but had not arrived as yet.

He finally did arrive—an hour after his wife had died…

* * *

The six days before the funeral were the worst of Sally's life—though for once her father rose to the occasion and looked after the arrangements. Devastated by her mum's death, even though it had been expected, Sally cried herself to sleep every night. Tossing and turning in bed, she remembered how Zac had once offered to cuddle her, and, oh, how she longed for the comfort and the strength of his strong arms now.

The funeral was held on a bright July day at the church in Bournemouth where her mum had been baptised, a short forty-three years earlier. The service was brief and the congregation was no more than fifty people. Her doctor and the nurse who had been her primary carer at the home came; the rest were friends and people her mum had known all her life, plus Al and his parents, and Sally was glad of their support. But in her heart of hearts she wished Zac was by her side, supporting her. A futile wish as there had been no word from him…no call…

Her father played the grieving widower, but she was too distraught with grief to care what he did.

Her mother was buried in the cemetery in a plot next to her parents, and the funeral tea was held in the hotel where Sally and her father were staying for the night.

The whole affair took barely four hours, from start to finish.

She could not face dinner with her father, but the next morning he handed Sally her mother's jewellery box with the statement, 'She left you this. You can check with the solicitor, if you like, but what money she had she left to me. As for the studio apartment, you can keep it until probate is settled and there is no danger of it being included in your mother's estate, and then I want it back.' He said this without a trace of shame, and then got into a new BMW car and drove off.

Sally had no desire to return to her apartment, but it was legally hers and she was damned sure she was not giving it back to her father. That he could suggest such a thing at her mum's funeral beggared belief. He must think she really was the silly girl he was fond of calling her, as easily manipulated as her mother had been. He was so self-centred, so blind, he didn't realise she had only ever obeyed him for her mum's sake…

Well, not any more… She was desolate with grief, and had never felt so alone in her life, but she was not a fool…

At Al's insistence she spent a few days at his parents' home. In comfort, with old friends around her, she began to come to terms with her mum's death. And with Al's encouragement she decided she was going to take a sabbatical from her job and see the world, as she had once promised herself.

She walked into her apartment a week later, full of good intentions. The first one was to have a strong cup of coffee after the long car journey. She saw the message light flashing on the telephone as she filled the kettle at the sink.

Zac, she thought, and her heart missed a beat. It was over four long, devastatingly sad weeks since she had seen him, but she was wrong. There were two messages: in the first no one spoke—probably a wrong number—and the second message was from the estate agent who was handling the sale of her apartment, asking her to get in touch immediately. He had a cash buyer for the property at the full asking price, on condition she left the furniture and could complete and vacate within two weeks…

August in Peru, and spring was on the horizon. Sally breathed in the warm air and felt her excitement mounting as she boarded the bus outside Lima airport with the other members of her tour group, embarking on a month-long tour of the country.

She still thought of her mum every day, and the sadness would be with her always, Sally knew, but it would no longer rule her life. She thought of Zac most days as well, but she was gradually coming to terms with their one-week affair, having accepted that that was all it had ever been or could have been with a womaniser like Zac.

Today was her birthday: she was twenty-six and free to do exactly what she wanted, with no one to worry about except herself for the first time in years.

Actually, it had been surprisingly easy to leave London. The sale of her apartment had gone through without a hitch, she had sold her car, and with her clothes and the few belongings she wanted to keep she had stayed with Jemma for a week until her holiday started. Jemma was storing her things for her, and Sally now had more money than she had ever dreamt of. She would buy somewhere to live eventually—but not yet.

Her boss had agreed to her taking a year-long sabbatical, and the world was her oyster. If some nights she woke from sleep with dreams of Zac Delucca still haunting her she dismissed them from her mind—usually by making a cup of hot choco-late. It was now seven weeks since they had parted—not that she was counting!

Sally's blue eyes widened in awe as she stood high in the Andes, the ruins of Machu Picchu spread out before her. She had made it, her dream come true, and with the other members of the party she followed where the guide led.

It was everything and more that she had ever imagined, and she would have liked to spend some time to explore on her own, but when they stopped for morning coffee to her embarrassment she fainted... The youngest and probably the fittest member of the party, and yet she was the only one affected by the thin air—or so she thought...

Zac Delucca ran his hands through his hair. He could not concentrate on the papers before him, and, spinning around in his chair, he stared out of the window of his office, looking out over Rome and seeing nothing but the image of Sally. He had lost count of the times he had reached for his phone to call her and put it down again. Once he had actually let it ring and had got her answering service; he hadn't left a message. And Lisa in Milan was a lost cause, because he had no desire to bed the woman—or any woman except Sally, which was a first for him.

Salmacis, the nymph of the fountain, he thought with a wry smile. If she had been anything like her namesake Sally then poor Hermaphroditos hadn't stood a chance but to become one with her...

Finally Zac had to accept that he felt as if he had become one with Sally in a way he had never considered possible before. She had totally bewitched him. From the night she drew blood from his arm with the roses, and then lay naked in his arms, he had fallen under her spell, and now he felt as if she was drawing the life blood from his body. He couldn't concentrate on work; he couldn't think straight for any length of time. His waking and sleeping hours were filled with images of his Salmacis.

The door opened and Zac swung back. 'I ordered that I was not to be disturbed,' he growled as Raffe walked into the room and sat down in a chair facing the desk. 'I hired you to take care of things. What's gone wrong now?'

'Nothing—except you. According to Anna, your secretary, you are impossible to work with and someone has to tell you. I have been given the task. For the past four months you have travelled constantly and driven all your staff crazy—both here and in America. Not to mention the Far East, where apparently your abrupt attitude so insulted the head of the Japanese company we were in the process of buying that he has just informed me he is pulling out of the deal. What is going on with you, Zac? Woman trouble…?'

'I don't *have* women trouble,' Zac said adamantly, and knew he lied. He also knew he could not go on like this.

He had never been close to anyone in his life except maybe Raffe and Marco, his old fight manager, who now, with his wife, took care of his home in Calabria. They were as near to family as he had. He was a loner, and he had never needed anyone before, but now he needed Sally Paxton every which way there was…

He had been a coward too long. He loved Sally, and he wanted her bound to him by every law known to man—including marriage, he decided, and he was going to make it happen.

'Well, something is bugging you.' Raffe interrupted his musing. 'And the sooner you get over it the better for everyone. Anyway, back to business. I have just come back from London and everything is going smoothly and very profitably. A new contract has been signed to provide the Saudi Arabian government with the components they want.'

'Good. And Paxton? Is he behaving himself?' Zac asked, in the hope that Sally might be mentioned. Not that it mattered. His mind was made up: he was going to London to get her…

'Yes, though I never did understand why you kept him on just because his wife was in a nursing home. You are not usually so generous to a thief. Actually, it is immaterial now, as apparently his wife died a few months back. He took a couple of weeks' compassionate leave and returned to work, so there is nothing to stop you firing him now, which is no more than he deserves.'

'And his daughter?' Zac demanded, leaping to

his feet. 'Sally? Has anyone been in touch with her? Offered our sympathy? Anything at all?'

'I should have guessed!' Raffe exclaimed. 'The short temper, the irritability—it all makes sense. Your problem is the very lovely daughter, and that is why you let Paxton stay. I'm right, aren't I?'

Zac gave him a quelling look. 'Shut up, Raffe, and order the jet. I'm going to London.'

Five days later Zac walked out of the British Museum, almost defeated. Sally appeared to have vanished off the face of the earth. His first shock had been the discovery that she had sold the apartment and left no forwarding address. The estate agent who had handled the sale had been no help, except to tell him the apartment had been on the market for a couple of months. Sally had never mentioned the fact, but he realised now where she had hoped to get the money from to pay him back, which made him feel even worse.

He'd had a long talk with her father, but he had no idea where she had gone and didn't care. Her boss had informed him she was on a year's sabbatical. He had not heard from her yet, but she had said she would keep in touch. Finally Zac had swallowed his pride and contacted Al, and he had told him Sally had left to go on a month-long tour of

Peru. But that had been over a couple of months ago, and he had no idea where she was going afterwards.

Zac paused by the Bentley, the lines of strain etched deep in his face as he pondered on what to do next. He had called on her boss a second time in the hopes he might have heard from Sally, but no joy. A private detective was the next step, he decided, and was about to get in the car when a young woman approached him.

'Excuse me, but are you Mr Delucca?'

He was going to ignore her—until she added, 'My boss told me you were looking for my friend Sally…'

Sally didn't notice the big black car parked fifty yards further up the road as she turned her car into the drive and stopped. She slid out and picked up her shopping bag, which contained the new phone she had purchased along with other items. There was a smile on her face as she walked up the short garden path to the cottage she had rented in the seaside town of Littlehampton. Once, as a six-year-old, she had spent a weekend in a hotel here, with her mother and her grandma, and it was one of the most treasured memories she had of her childhood.

Her whole life had changed from the moment she had fainted at the ruins of Machu Picchu. Joan Adams, a retired doctor she had got to know well as they were the only single females travelling with the group, had pointed out that it was unlikely the thinness of the air had affected a fit young woman like her, and had suggested she might be pregnant. At first Sally had denied the possibility, but as the tour had continued and the morning sickness had started, Sally had had to reconsider.

She had thought long and hard on the flight back to England. Further travelling abroad was out for the foreseeable future, she'd decided, but that did not mean she had to stay in London.

Jemma had let her stay with her for the time it took Sally to buy a new car and pack up most of her belongings, and had accepted Sally's excuse that rather than travelling abroad she wanted to see more of her own country.

She had spotted a picture of the cottage in Littlehampton in the window of an estate agent in the nearby town of Worthing: for sale or to let unfurnished, with great sea views. Sally had viewed it on impulse, and taken a twelve-month lease on it the next day.

She opened the door and walked into the hall, hung up her coat and, dropping her shopping bag in the living room, she went to the kitchen to make a cup of tea. It was amazing, she thought, how life could take with one hand and give back with the other. She had lost her mum, but was soon going to *be* a mum…

She had registered with a local GP, and had her first scan at the hospital in Worthing. The baby was well, and the precious picture from the scan was in a picture frame at her bedside. If the baby was a girl she was going to call her Pamela, after her mum; if it was a boy... She hadn't decided... And she hadn't decided when she would tell Zac Delucca either.

She made a cup of tea and carried it through into the living room. She placed it on the table at the side of the nearest of the two cream soft-cushioned sofas she had bought that flanked the fireplace. She had opted for side-tables rather than a centre one, to give the illusion of space. Kicking off her shoes and sitting down, she curled her feet up on the sofa and reached for her teacup.

Sipping the hot tea, she supposed she would have to tell Zac Delucca some day—a man had a right to know he had fathered a child—but not yet... Maybe after the birth...

She wanted to savour every minute of her pregnancy in peace, and there was nothing peaceful about Zac Delucca. He went through life like a tornado, sweeping up anything he wanted and discarding the rest. Telling him could wait...

She glanced around the room. The warm, peach-painted walls, the oak ceiling beams and the polished oak floor looked sturdy and timeless, and the large peach, green and cream rug she had bought to put between the two sofas added a cosy touch. She had enjoyed choosing and purchasing the furniture for the living room and main bedroom. The second bedroom was for the baby and she had yet to start on that.

She was into nesting in a big way, she thought happily, and with a year's lease and the opportunity to buy if she wished she had left all her options open. If she decided to go back to her job in London at the end of her sabbatical she could. Or she could stay here. In the meantime all she had to concentrate on was her baby. With a contented sigh she reached for her shopping and withdrew the box containing her new phone and put it to one side. Then she took out the package containing the baby garments she had bought. She laid the tiny yellow booties and matching hat and jacket on the table, a soft smile curving her lips. It turned into a frown as the doorbell sounded. Reluctantly she got to her feet, padded into the small hall and opened the door...

CHAPTER THIRTEEN

SALLY's mouth fell open, her eyes widening in stunned disbelief on the man standing before her. It couldn't be... It wasn't possible... But it was Zac Delucca...

She grasped the doorjamb, her legs suddenly weak and her heartbeat thundering in her breast, and she could not stop the heated rush of awareness flooding through her body as she looked up into his darkly handsome face. She had convinced herself she was over the hateful man, and she had certainly never *loved* him. That had been a momentary aberration brought about by sex, nothing more. She was content with her new life—and yet just the sight of him made a mockery of her hard-won serenity.

No, she would not allow herself to think that way. She straightened up, squaring her slender shoulders; it was probably her hormones running riot—something her doctor had warned her about—nothing more...

* * *

'Hello, Sally.' Zac could barely speak as he drank in the sight of Sally with hungry eyes. She stood in the doorway, her glorious red curls falling around her shoulders, her surprise evident in the shocked expression on her face, and emotion clogged his throat.

He looked and looked again. He would not have thought it possible, but she was even more beautiful than he remembered. The almost constant hint of sadness in her brilliant eyes and the faint shadows underneath them had faded away. Her beautiful face was free of make-up and her silken skin glowed with health.

She was wearing a fine blue sweater that clung lovingly to her full breasts, and a hip-hugging, gently flaring skirt that stopped just below her knees, showing a tempting glimpse of her fabulous legs. Her bare feet with pink-tipped toes were almost his undoing, and he had to battle to control his surging flesh. Sally was the most overtly feminine woman he had ever known. He had never seen her wear a pair of jeans or trousers, like the majority of women her age. Apart from the pink velvet lounging suit… No. He didn't dare go there. The memory of her removing it and what had followed was too vivid, and he would not be able to stop himself reaching for her.

'Zac—what are you doing here?'

Her voice was just the same: slightly husky, with a low timbre, her pronunciation precise—probably a result of losing her stutter, he realised. And it was corny, but true; it was music to his ears.

'A concerned friend of yours, Jemma, asked me to look you up.'

'Jemma?' Sally had phoned Jemma twice since she had left London, the last time just after she had booked into a hotel outside Littlehampton, but not since—mainly because she had only replaced her lost phone today.

'But she can't have known my new address, so how did you find me?' Wondering what evil trick of fate had brought him here, she was trying valiantly to remain calm while her heart was still pounding like a drum in her chest.

'It is cold out here. Ask me in—I need a drink,' Zac commanded, ignoring her question. Surprisingly, he was more afraid than he had ever been in his life. He could hardly blurt out that he had tracked her down because he loved her and wanted her back—not after the way he had treated her before… She would never believe him. He had made enough mistakes with Sally, and this time he was determined to do it right. Romance her, date her, grovel if he had to. And sex could wait until she came to him of her own free will.

Sally swallowed hard. Slowly recovering from the shock of seeing Zac, and her own instant reaction to him, she began to note the change in him. His face was thinner, the grooves from nose to mouth more deeply etched, and the lines of strain around his eyes were plainly discernible. The cashmere overcoat he wore appeared to hang loosely on his broad frame. Realising she was staring, she stepped nervously back and indicated with her hand that he should enter, taking care that he did not touch her as he moved into the hall.

'The kitchen is this way…' she began, but she was too late. He had already walked into the living room.

Swiftly she followed him as she realised what he might see. She reached for the baby clothes she had left on the table, but again she was too late. He had picked up the tiny yellow jacket…

'Give that to me.' She held out her hand, her face burning. 'I'll put this stuff away and make you a cup of coffee. You said you were cold. October can be chilly…' She was babbling, she knew, but she didn't seem able to stop.

'Enough, Sally,' he snapped, catching her hand. 'Baby clothes? Who for? You?' he queried, his eyes narrowed on her scarlet face.

'So what if they are?' she snapped back. She would not lie and deny her baby. Pulling her hand free, she gathered the garments up and shoved them back in the bag. 'It is none of your business.'

Her reply ignited a furious anger in Zac as it hit him that she must be pregnant—and the child could not be his; he had always used protection. No wonder he had thought she looked glowing. While he had spent months aching for her, Sally must have gone straight from his bed into the arms of another man.

The thought of Sally with another man cut him to the bone. She had responded to him in spite of the disgust she felt at his tactics, in spite of her declared hatred of him. In his arrogant conceit he had thought her responsive body was enough for him, and too late he had realised differently.

He had taken her innocence, made her aware of the pleasures of the flesh and left. In fact, he scathingly reminded himself, he had let guilt get the better of him and decided it was the right thing to do—for her sake. What an idiot… He should have taken his fill of her and to hell with his conscience…

He let his gaze sweep contemptuously over her and noted the subtle changes to her body. Her waist was not so clearly defined, and her high, firm breasts appeared fuller. His attention returned to her face. She was watching him with wide, wary eyes, and she had a right to be afraid at this moment. He felt like wringing her slender neck.

'So who is the father?' he sneered. 'Or don't you know? As I recall you were a very eager pupil, but I thought I had taught you better. You should have remembered protection. I always did—even when you were gagging for it.'

Sally saw red. Her hand flew out and connected with his face, knocking his head sideways. 'You sanctimonious bastard! Mister bloody perfect,' she swore—something she never did. 'Well, you are not that clever. My baby was conceived on the nineteenth of June, so work it out for yourself and get out.'

His cheek stinging, Zac raised his hand to catch hers—and dropped it as the import of her words sank into his head. That was the date of the first night he had made love to her. He knew because it was burnt like a brand into his mind for all time. Recalling that night now, he remembered that the second time he had made love to her had initially been in an anger-driven passion because of that word.

'Fine…' he murmured, and all the colour drained from his face. She was right—he had forgotten to use protection. Sally was pregnant with his child. He was going to be a father and it was one hell of a shock. But Zac, being the man he was, although reeling from the knowledge, did not stop considering all the options, and swiftly he realised Sally's pregnancy solved all his problems. He could not have planned it better if he had tried.

He wanted Sally any way he could get her, and this would cut out any need to grovel—not something he had ever done before. Now he would not have to. In fact, she would probably be delighted and grateful when he told her he was prepared to marry her, and the idea of having a baby was growing on him by the minute… A son and heir…

'Good. I'm glad we agree. So go.' She was walking back into the hall, but he reached out and caught her shoulder, spinning her around to face him.

'You misunderstood, Sally. I am not going anywhere, *cara*.' He smiled. 'Obviously you and I need to talk. Discovering you are pregnant with my baby has come as quite a shock. My first reaction was less than gallant, I admit, but the thought of you with another man did nothing for my temper. I want you to know I accept totally the child you are carrying is mine, and naturally I will marry you as quickly as it can be arranged.'

If Zac had expected her grateful acceptance, that was not what he got.

Stunned, Sally looked at him. He was smiling. Zac was actually smiling, and confidently expecting her to accept his magnanimous offer. With a terrific effort of self-control she resisted the temptation to slap the grin off his face.

'I think I may have told you this once before,' she said, with no trace of the anger and the turmoil he had caused visible in the cool blue eyes she lifted to his. 'But I'll say it again so there can be no doubt in your mind. I wouldn't marry you in a million years,' she drawled sarcastically.

Zac had gone pale when she'd said the baby was his, but now his face flushed dark with anger. True to form, then… They always ended up fighting, and she didn't need the hassle in her present state. Shrugging his hands from her shoulders, she took a few steps back.

'If I had not turned up today were you ever going to tell me you were pregnant?' he demanded harshly.

'I hadn't given it much thought.'

'I don't believe you. Any woman who discovers she is pregnant is naturally going to think of the father and what genes her child might inherit.'

He was right—but then Zac always thought he was right. It infuriated Sally, and she told him the truth.

'I wanted to enjoy my pregnancy, relaxed and free of stress, and as you are the least restful person I know I decided on balance it was better to put off telling you straight away. But I would have told you eventually. I was thinking probably after my baby is born.'

'After?' His rapier-like glance raked her from head to toe, as though he had never seen her before, and in one stride he was towering over her. 'You were *thinking* about telling me *after* my child was born?' he prompted incredulously. 'How long after? One year? Two? Ten?' he drawled, and, reaching for her, he hauled her hard against him.

Her eyes widened at the icy anger in his tone. His dark gaze caught and held hers and she was powerless to break the contact.

'Well, listen to me now, Sally Paxton. I am doing the thinking for both of us from now on. No child of mine will be born out of wedlock. You *will* marry me, and our child *will* have two parents.'

'No,' she bit out between clenched teeth. 'I won't marry you. But I will allow you visiting rights,' she conceded determined to hang onto her temper and stay calm and reasonable. But she was equally determined not to allow Zac to walk all over her.

'If anyone gets visiting rights it will be you, because I fully intend for my child to live with *me*. I will file for custody the second it leaves your womb.'

'You won't get it,' she shot back. 'This is England—the mother almost always gets custody.'

'Not quite right. Britain is part of the European community, and I will tie you up in the courts here and in Europe for years. Is that what you want for our child?'

'You would do that?' Sally asked, and saw the implacable determination in his dark eyes. Suddenly she was more afraid than angry.

'Yes.' His hands slipped from her shoulders, but before she could move his arms wrapped around her, one hand splayed across the base of her spine, bringing her into close contact with his large body. 'But it does not have to be that way, Sally.'

Her breasts tightened against the soft wool of her sweater in agitation—or so she told herself. But to her shame the pressure of his strong thighs against her was arousing other more basic emotions. She curled her hands on his forearms in an attempt to keep some space between them, but it didn't help...

'Be reasonable, Sally.' He glanced down to where her swollen nipples were clearly outlined by the fine wool of her jumper, then back to her face. 'Sexually we are more than compatible—we are totally combustible,' he said wryly. 'And all marriages are a money-based transaction and I have a limitless amount. Whether I spend a fortune fighting you in court, or you marry me and gain the benefit of unlimited wealth for yourself and our child, it is up to you to decide, but either way I will win in the end. I always do.'

Sally looked searchingly at him. The tension in the room was palpable. Her decision, he had said... She either married him or consigned her as yet unborn child to growing up in the midst of a battle between two warring parents. A far from ideal scenario, she knew, but the idea of marriage terrified her. She was only four months pregnant, and no matter what Zac threatened she had plenty of time to make a decision.

'Then I will see you in court,' she answered spitefully.

She saw the surprise and anger in his eyes, and his arms fell to his sides and she was free.

'Now I want you to leave.'

'Not before you give me the coffee you promised… I am frozen in shock, and it is the least you can do seeing as I have given you a child,' he drawled mockingly.

Torn between good manners and a desire to be rid of him, she hesitated. Good manners won as he added, 'Please…'

'Have a seat.' She indicated the sofa. 'I'll make you a coffee and then you can leave.' And, turning, she entered the kitchen.

Sally switched on the kettle and put her hands flat on the worktop, her head bent. She had managed to hold her own with Zac, but only just… Being in his company, talking to him—mostly arguing, she amended—had brought a host of painfully suppressed emotions bubbling to the surface, and being held in his arms had almost been her undoing.

She lifted her head and stared out of the window at the garden and the rolling fields beyond. She took a few deep, steadying breaths, striving to calm her fast-beating heart and slowly rising temper. That he had the gall to turn up out of the blue and then demand she marry him was unbelievable.

But stress was not good for the baby, and she continued to breathe deeply.

She had half expected Zac to follow her to the kitchen—she wasn't blind; he was as mad as hell beneath that mocking exterior—but surprisingly he didn't. The kettle boiled, and she made a mug of instant coffee for him, and a cup of tea for herself. She placed a few biscuits on a plate and put the lot on a tray. But she was reluctant to face Zac again.

A deep, shuddering sigh escaped her. She couldn't hide in the kitchen much longer, and Zac was right in a way: they *would* have to talk eventually. Her baby deserved to know its father. But then, thinking of her own father, she was not absolutely convinced that was true, and on that thought she walked back into the living room.

CHAPTER FOURTEEN

SALLY walked straight past Zac to place the tray on the opposite side table. She picked up the coffee mug and turned to look at him, and her hand froze in mid-air.

He had removed his overcoat and was wearing a black sweater and matching pants. Sitting on the sofa with his shoulders hunched, his elbows resting on his knees and holding his head in his hands, the arrogant Zac Delucca looked utterly exhausted. As she stared he lifted his head and ran his hands distractedly through his now over-long hair.

'Are you all right?' she asked, concerned though she did not want to be. She had never seen him look anything other than vibrant and totally in control until now. At her query he raised his eyes, and she saw uncertainty and pain mingled in the black depths as they met hers.

'No, not really, Sally,' he admitted surprisingly. 'I have been sitting here thinking of our past relationship and the mess I made of it while you were in the kitchen.'

'Your coffee,' she said swiftly, and handed him the china mug. She didn't want to talk about their brief affair; it hurt too much…

'Thank you.' His long fingers brushed hers as he took the mug, setting off an unwanted frisson of awareness through her body, and swiftly she stepped back.

'Instant, I'm afraid,' she told him, and sat on the sofa opposite. 'I ran out of the real stuff some time ago, and as I don't drink coffee any more…' she trailed off.

'It will do.' She watched as he lifted the mug to his lips and took a swallow. 'Maybe not.' He grimaced, replacing the mug on the table. Glancing across at her, he added, 'Have you anything stronger? Whisky? Wine, perhaps?'

'No. I don't drink because of the baby.'

'Ah, yes…our baby,' he remarked softly.

Sally recognised his anger had abated, but she had a sneaking suspicion a low-voiced Zac was a lot more dangerous.

'You must really hate me, Sally, if you are prepared to fight me in court for our child. I would never have done it, but my temper got the better of me. The perceived wisdom is that two parents are the ideal, but, being brought up in an orphanage, I would have thanked my lucky stars to have even one loving parent.'

Zac could say that now, and perhaps he meant it, but she didn't trust him and she didn't bother responding. Instead she picked up her cup of tea to take a drink. Actually, she had no intention of fighting him over the baby; she just needed breathing space to think of an acceptable alternative— preferably another five months... But she saw no reason to tell Zac. Let him suffer... After all, she had suffered enough at his hands... *Liar,* a tiny devil in her head whispered. *You loved his hands all over you.*

Abruptly she replaced the cup on the saucer and smoothed the fabric of her skirt down her thighs in a nervous gesture. As the silence stretched between them the room suddenly seemed very small, the air heavy with tension. Sally was still shocked Zac had actually turned up here, and then she realised he had never answered her question as to how he knew where she lived.

'How did you find me? You never said,' she prompted.

'I was in London and I called at your apartment, thinking to offer you my condolences on the death of your mother. Belatedly, I know, but Raffe had only just informed me of the fact. I know more than most how much you did for your mother,' he said with a self-deprecating grimace. 'I know how much you loved her, and I am truly sorry for your loss.'

'Thank you,' Sally responded. 'But you still have not answered my question. How did you get my address?'

'When I called at your apartment building I was surprised to discover you had sold the place, and your father had no idea where you had gone. I called at the museum to see if your boss knew, and your friend Jemma accosted me as I left, and told me she was worried about you. Apparently, on your return from Peru you had stayed with her just long enough to buy a new car and take off on your travels around Britain. You had said you would call her every week, but apart from a couple of calls, the last from a hotel near here, she had heard nothing more and she had been unable to contact you for over a month.'

'I lost my phone—or it was stolen. I only replaced it today,' Sally interjected.

He glanced at the box on the table. 'So it would seem. Anyway, I told Jemma I would help her find you. A call to a detective agency with the name of the hotel you stayed at and I had your address within twenty-four hours.'

'Oh.'

'Oh? Is that all you have to say?' he asked quietly, his dark eyes holding hers. 'Aren't you in the least curious as to why I came instead of Jemma?'

'I never really gave you much thought.'

'I can't say I blame you.' He shook his dark head. 'I never gave you any consideration when I forced you into an affair, and for that I am truly sorry.'

Zac? Apologizing? What was wrong with the man? 'Forget it. I have,' she lied. This soft-spoken, caring Zac was doing strange things to her heart-rate.

'Damn it, Sally.' He got to his feet. 'I can't forget.' And he paced the length of the room, which for him was about six steps, looking strangely agitated. Then he dropped down beside her. She tried to get up, but he looped an arm around her waist and urged her back down. His contrite attitude hadn't lasted long, Sally thought, squirming to break free.

'Please, Sally, sit still and listen,' he demanded. 'I deserve that much, surely?'

She stopped struggling. He didn't deserve anything in her book, but he was too big to fight, and to be honest she was curious.

'I missed you like hell when we parted, Sally, and I realised I did not want to forget you—could not forget you.' His dark, serious eyes sought hers. 'Not then, not now, not ever.'

She looked away. 'If this is a trick to sweet-talk me into marrying you for the baby, forget it. My mum is dead. I owe you nothing,' she said bluntly. But with his hand curving around her waist, his long fingers resting on the side of her now rounded stomach and the warmth of his body against hers, he was arousing a host of old, familiar emotions.

'It is no trick, I swear. I had made up my mind to go to London and ask you to forgive me for being such an arrogant, overbearing idiot even before Raffe told me your mother had died. I used her death as an excuse when you asked me because I am no good at revealing my emotions. Not that I had many until I met you,' he said dryly. 'The moment I saw you enter Westwold that day, I wanted you with a passion I had never felt before. I smiled at you, and you didn't notice me.' He gave her a droll look. 'And I am quite large to overlook…'

'Dented your ego…?' she quipped, and met his eyes—which was a mistake. The warmth and the hint of vulnerability in the dark depths made her breath catch in her throat. Maybe, just maybe, he was telling the truth. A tiny flicker of hope ignited inside her. He no longer seemed quite the hard, overbearing Zac she had known, and though she did not want to marry him, they could perhaps come to some suitable arrangement.

'Yes. That and more. It was a salutary experience, and probably long overdue,' he admitted ruefully.

He sounded sincere, but Sally still didn't quite trust him—though she did give him an explanation. 'I was too worried about Mum to notice anything much that day. Her doctor had told me the weekend before she had not long left.'

Zac's arm tightened around her. 'Now I feel even worse.' He grimaced. 'I coerced you into being my lover at a really low point in your life, and I can only say sorry again, Sally. But I would be lying if I said I was sorry for making love to you. I think I fell in love with you on sight. My first thought was that you looked bridal… Maybe my subconscious was trying to tell me something even then.'

Sally drew in a deep, shocked breath. Maybe once she would have been ecstatic to hear Zac mention the *L* word, but now she was doubtful.

'From day one you confused me. I found myself changing my mind about you over and over again. But from our first kiss in the limousine I knew I had to make you mine.' He stopped and was silent for a while. 'The night I came to your apartment—the night you left me aching and frustrated and I stormed out—I was determined to have nothing more to do with you.'

'I gathered that,' Sally shot back smartly. 'I think it was you telling me to stick my head in the cooler box that convinced me.'

Zac's lips twitched in the beginnings of a smile. 'Not one of my better moments, Sally, and the only excuse I have is I was out of my mind with frustration. I wanted you so badly.' He caught her hand

and curled it in his own. 'But later, when we did make love, I realised why you stopped me. It was the understandable nerves of an innocent.'

Nerves of a not so innocent sort tightened at the warmth of the hand holding hers. Zac was getting to her, making her remember things she had tried to forget, and she tugged free.

'Wrong. I caught sight of the two of us in the mirrored wardrobe and was reminded of where I was. My dad's old love-nest. He graciously gave it to me at my mum's instigation, after persuading her to sell the family home so he could buy himself a much grander apartment in Notting Hill. Mum agreed because the insensitive swine actually told her it would help with death duties.'

It still enraged her even now when she thought about it, and once she'd got started Sally could not stop.

'I hated that apartment. The first week I moved in the phone never stopped ringing with women trying to contact him. I changed the number in the end, and painted the whole place, replaced his furniture with my own. But nothing could change what that studio was in my eyes. The only reason I set the guidelines on our deal to that apartment was because it never failed to remind me of the faithlessness of men, and was therefore entirely appropriate for what you had in mind.'

Sally had said too much. But digging over the past had aroused emotions she did not want to face. She just wanted Zac to leave, and she tried to rise.

'*Dio!*' Zac exclaimed. 'This just gets worse and worse. But they say confession is good for the soul, and you *are* going to let me finish, Sally.'

His arm tightened around her waist, the expression on his face one of grim determination.

'I had no intention of seeing you again after that night, but when you and Al walked into that restaurant the next night, I saw red. I was crazy with jealousy—a first for me… I was frantic. I wanted to walk over and rip his head off.'

There was no humour in his tone, but Sally had to bite back the laugh that bubbled up in her throat at his outrageous statement. She didn't think he would appreciate being laughed at.

'Instead I was sociable and polite, and you ignored me, then deliberately insulted me.'

'What did you expect? A medal?' Sally slotted in.

'Don't be facetious, Sally. I am serious. I was furious to the point of mindless rage with you, which was why I decided to use your father's dishonesty against you. I knew you responded to me, and I didn't care how I got you as long as I did. I behaved disgracefully, and I am thoroughly ashamed of my actions. But I can't be ashamed of the result. And, though I bitterly regret any hurt I caused you, I will never regret making love to you. It was the most amazing, memorable experience of my life and always will be. What I am trying to say, Sally, is that I love you, and I want to marry you, and I did long before I knew about the baby.'

Sally frowned, her blue eyes wide and wary, searching his face, looking for some sign that would convince her he was telling the truth. But with her parents as an example she had spent too long mistrusting love, and was too cynical about most men to immediately believe Zac.

'Humph!' she snorted 'You could have fooled me. You walked in here, and when you realised I was pregnant you insulted me, and then demanded I marry you. Why should I believe a word you say now? I remember our first limousine ride as well. When you told me you were not into commitment, and had no intention of ever marrying, but were up for an affair with no strings attached. So you will excuse me for believing your transformation from arrogant, commitment-shy ex-lover to soft-talking want-to-be husband is just a tad too convenient.'

'You don't believe me, and I deserve that. But Sally, if you will just give me another chance to let me prove how much I love you... I won't pressure you into making love as I did before, though it will be hell waiting. I need you, want you so much. You get under my skin like no other woman has ever done.'

At his mention of other woman Sally was brought back to reality with a thud. Margot's image loomed large in her mind. She reached for her cup and took a sip of tea to control her nerves before she responded.

'As for being the only woman to get under your skin—that is no great accolade, given how many get into your bed. Margot for one. You must take me for an idiot, Zac. You tried to seduce me on the Monday, took her to your bed on Tuesday, and blackmailed me into sex the following night.'

Sally watched his reaction and saw the effect her words had on him. His great body tensed and all the colour drained from his face, leaving him grey and looking older than his years.

'You really think so little of me that you believe I am capable of such deplorable behaviour?'

'I know so,' she said bluntly.

'I have never had sex with Margot in my life. In fact, you are the only woman I have made love to in well over a year,' he declared outrageously.

He actually sounded sincere, Sally thought bitterly. Going by her own limited experience with Zac, he was a highly sexed, three or four times a night man. Zac celibate for over a year was a joke… Why was she wasting her time listening to him?

'I found her black hairband, clips and perfume in the cabinet in your bathroom. So don't bother to lie.'

For a moment he was silent, his brows drawn together in a frown. That had stopped his fairy tale of love and marriage, Sally thought cynically.

Then suddenly he threw his head back, a broad grin lighting his face. 'So that is why the last night we were together you changed from my Salmacis, my dream lover, to a cold-eyed witch,' he declared. Taking her cup from her hand, he placed it on the table, and with his other around her waist tugged her towards him.

'What…?' was as far as Sally got as he kissed her with a hungry, driven passion that knocked the breath from her body. The suddenness of his action gave her no time to build a defence, and she reacted with helpless hunger to the pressure of his mouth, welcomed the thrust of his tongue with her own.

Her instinctive response was all the encouragement he needed to continue, with a heady sensuality that drove her almost mindless. He groaned and lifted her bodily onto his lap, his arms like steel bands around her. The swiftness of his action, the tightness of his hold, the sudden awareness of his intensely aroused body, brought her back to her senses, and she flung back her head.

'Stop it, Zac,' she gasped, pushing at his chest. 'Let go of me.'

'Never,' he said.

But surprisingly, he did slacken his hold on her, and jerkily Sally slid back onto the sofa. But one arm remained gently yet firmly around her waist, preventing her moving any further away.

Breathless, she brushed the hair out of her eyes and glared angrily at him. 'What did you do that for?'

'I had to.' He grinned: a broad smile, revealing his perfect white teeth. 'Because you gave me the first glimmer of hope I have had in months,' he said, totally unrepentant.

'Me?' She was confused, and still shaken from the assault on her senses.

'Yes. I realised you were crazy jealous because you thought I had made love to Margot.'

'Don't flatter yourself,' she huffed, but without much force.

'I wouldn't dare with you,' he said dryly. 'You have the ability to chop me off at the knees with a glance. But I was telling you the truth before, Sally. And as for the stuff you found in the bathroom cabinet, Raffe and his very attractive black-haired wife were using the apartment while he worked on the transition at Westwold. After I arrived he went back to Italy on the Monday, and I moved in. It is a company apartment—not only for my use.'

'Oh.' Sally felt a fool. 'I didn't know Raffe Costa was married.'

'He has been for five years, and they are desperate for a child.' This time his smile was rueful. 'I think he will be pleased for us, but hardly ecstatic given the circumstances.'

'There is no us,' she said automatically, but now she wasn't quite so adamant. If she had known what she knew now that night in the apartment, would she have been so nasty to Zac?

'Oh, yes, there is, Sally,' Zac assured her in a husky tone. And, turning towards her, he ran his long fingers through the silken fall of her hair to cup the back of her head in his strong hand. 'And you *are* going to marry me,' Zac told her in a firm voice. 'After we parted I spent the most miserable few months of my life, worrying about what you were doing and who you were with. I had the most dreadful nightmares. I'd wake up in the night sweating, imagining you with another man. Or I'd dream you were in my arms and wake up devastated to be without you... I am not going through that again, and I am not going anywhere until you promise to marry me.'

Sally looked at him uncertainly. Had he really suffered so much without her? She saw the strain in his face and lifted a finger to trace the deep groove from his nose to his mouth. She looked into his eyes and saw he was deadly serious.

'You once told me you wanted three children

while you were young enough to enjoy them. Think about it, Sally. Do you want this baby to be an only child, like you and I were, or to have a few siblings to play with?'

'I did not mean that. I was only trying to put you off.'

'You didn't succeed.' And, taking his arm from her waist, he tilted her head back against the soft cushion. He withdrew his hand and stood up. He stared down at her, as though searching for words, and then slipped his hand into his pants pocket.

'I know you, Sally, and I'd bet my life it never occurred to you to get rid of this baby—though plenty of women would.'

'You'd win that bet.'

'I also know that with your father as an example marriage might scare you.' To her utter amazement he dropped down on one knee and, taking her hand in his other hand, he produced a small square box. 'Sally, my Salmacis, please, will you marry me? I love you, and I swear I will never betray you.'

He opened the box to reveal a brilliant sapphire and diamond ring.

'I am not asking you to love me, but to let me love you, as your husband, and who knows…?'

Sally looked into his eyes and saw the glimmer of moisture that could not dim the blaze of love and sincerity in the dark depths. Suddenly the defences she had built around her heart for years cracked wide-open, a flood of emotion pouring out, and she said, 'Yes.'

With an Italian sound of exultation, Zac grasped her hand and slipped the ring on her finger, then pulled her down beside him and kissed her with deep, profound tenderness and a love that touched her soul.

Sally's new rug was very convenient, as were the cushions from the sofa. With gentle, shaking hands he undressed her and shed his own clothes. He kissed her again, his hands cupping and caressing the fullness of her breasts and then stroking lower to cradle the still small mound of her tummy. She looked at him and saw the wonder, the awe in his eyes, before he bent his head to press a kiss on her stomach and his child.

He lifted his head, his dark eyes seeking hers. 'I won't hurt you or the baby, will I?' he asked.

Sally smiled softly. For once her magnificent, arrogant man did not have all the answers. She responded by reaching for him, her hands curving around his broad shoulders and pulling him down to her. 'No. I am past the first trimester—it is *fine*…' She accentuated the last word and smiled.

With a shout of joy mingled with relief Zac began to make love to her, with a gentle but tender and passionate intensity that surpassed anything that had gone before. Sally gave herself eagerly, and when Zac finally claimed her as his once more, she arched up to meet him, and they became one in a sunburst of love and life…

EPILOGUE

Sɪxᴛᴇᴇɴ months later Sally stood in the nursery of their home in Calabria, looking into the cot where Francesco, their son, was finally sleeping after an exciting day.

She had married Zac in a quiet Christmas wedding at the small church in Villa San Giovanni, the nearest town to his home in the countryside. Zac had insisted she wear white, despite her swelling belly, and the guest list on her side had been Jemma, and Charles and his wife and family, but not her father. Zac had had Raffe and his wife, who had just discovered she was pregnant, Marco and his wife, and a few local friends and employees.

Francesco had arrived on a beautiful spring day in March, just like today, and was a joy to behold. Sally reached down into the cot and stroked his black curly hair with a gentle hand. He was the image of his father, and just looking at him was enough to make her heart overflow with love and happiness. Today had been his first birthday, and they had thrown a party for a dozen children, from the ages of a few months to ten years old.

Zac had supposedly been in control of the party. But he had been a bigger hit than the troupe of clowns and jugglers he had hired to entertain the children. Francesco had ridden around on his shoulders, and so had most of the other children. And a riotous game of football, beloved of all Italians, had mostly consisted of Zac running after the ball as the youngsters kicked anywhere and everywhere. Now he was lying in the huge bath in their en suite bathroom, trying to ease his aching bones.

It seemed incredible to her now that she had ever doubted Zac or been afraid of marriage. He was a wonderful husband, and a devoted father who adored his son. Totally the opposite of her own father, who had married a woman thirty-five years younger than himself within six months of her mum's death and retired to Spain. Who said crime didn't pay? she thought, but without the anger and bitterness that had plagued her before. She had accepted that he had never been cut out to be a father, or faithful, and if anything she pitied his new wife…

Zac had told her about her father at the same time as he told her he had sold Westwold Components, because he knew she did not approve of the arms business. He had also added that the office gossip was the woman had married her dad for his money, and would leave him just as quickly when the cash ran out... What goes around comes around, Sally thought, and she didn't care any more.

She had her own family, and sometimes Sally could hardly believe how blessed she was. Zac had cut back on his workload and they spent most of their time here in Calabria. She had fallen in love with the house the moment she had seen it.

The original two-hundred-year-old farmhouse was only part of one wing now. If Zac wanted something he got it, and he had used the same approach to the house. It was a great rambling home now, with a gym and a swimming pool, six en suite bedrooms and an amazing master bedroom that had panoramic views across the Strait of Messina to Sicily and the toe of Italy. The building had evolved over the years to sit perfectly in the surrounding landscape of olive groves, cliffs and sea, though it would probably never win any prizes for architectural beauty.

She loved the house, and she loved Zac—but, strange as it seemed, she had never actually said the words. Maybe it was time she did...

Sally bent down to drop a kiss on Francesco's head.

Straightening, she felt two arms close around her waist.

'Is he asleep?' Zac murmured, looking over her head at his son sleeping in the cot. 'He looks like an angel. *Dio,* don't you just love him?'

Sally turned in his arms and linked hers around his neck. He was wearing only a towel slung around his lean hips and a smile to warm her heart—and quite a few other parts of her anatomy.

'Yes. And if you have recovered from the party, I thought I would take you to bed and show you how much I love *you*, Zac.'

His dark eyes flared with a luminous light, and he groaned as he pulled her against him, his sensuous mouth kissing every one of her delicate features before claiming her mouth in a deep, loving kiss.

'Thank you for that, *cara mia,*' he murmured, holding her close. 'I was beginning to worry you would never say the words I longed to hear, even though I know you feel them.'

'Conceited devil.' She grinned 'But I do love you.'

'No, not conceited—just a man who loves you to distraction. Now, what were you saying about taking me to bed…?' And, curving an arm around her waist, he led her quietly out of the nursery.

'I was thinking today,' he said as they walked towards their suite. 'If you agree, maybe it is time we started trying for the second of those three children you insisted you wanted when we met.'

'You are never going to let me forget that, Zac.'
They both laughed.

And then they wandered off to make a start on extending their family.

* * * * *

*Harlequin Intrigue top author Delores Fossen
presents a brand-new series of breathtaking
romantic suspense!*
TEXAS MATERNITY: HOSTAGES
The first installment available May 2010:
THE BABY'S GUARDIAN

Shaw cursed and hooked his arm around Sabrina.

Despite the urgency that the deadly gunfire created, he tried to be careful with her, and he took the brunt of the fall when he pulled her to the ground. His shoulder hit hard, but he held on tight to his gun so that it wouldn't be jarred from his hand.

Shaw didn't stop there. He crawled over Sabrina, sheltering her pregnant belly with his body, and he came up ready to return fire.

This was obviously a situation he'd wanted to avoid at all cost. He didn't want his baby in the middle of a fight with these armed fugitives, but when they fired that shot, they'd left him no choice. Now, the trick was to get Sabrina safely out of there.

"Get down," someone on the SWAT team yelled from the roof of the adjacent building.

Shaw did. He dropped lower, covering Sabrina as best he could.

There was another shot, but this one came from

a rifleman on the SWAT team. Shaw didn't look up, but he heard the sound of glass being blown apart.

The shots continued, all coming from his men, which meant it might be time to try to get Sabrina to better cover. Shaw glanced at the front of the building.

So that Sabrina's pregnant belly wouldn't be smashed against the ground, Shaw eased off her and moved her to a sitting position so that her back was against the brick wall. They were close. Too close. And face-to-face.

He found himself staring right into those sea-green eyes.

How will Shaw get Sabrina out?
Follow the daring rescue and the heartbreaking
aftermath in THE BABY'S GUARDIAN
by Delores Fossen,
available May 2010 from Harlequin Intrigue.

Copyright © 2010 by Delores Fossen

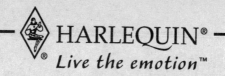

HARLEQUIN®
Live the emotion™

The series you love are now available in

LARGER PRINT!

The books are complete and unabridged—
printed in a larger type size to make it
easier on your eyes.

HARLEQUIN® *Romance*

From the Heart, For the Heart

HARLEQUIN® INTRIGUE®

Breathtaking Romantic Suspense

HARLEQUIN® *Presents*®

Seduction and Passion Guaranteed!

HARLEQUIN® *Super Romance*®

Exciting, Emotional, Unexpected

Try LARGER PRINT today!
Visit: www.eHarlequin.com
Call: 1-800-873-8635

LPDIR09

HARLEQUIN® *Romance*®

The rush of falling in love

Cosmopolitan
international settings

Believable, feel-good stories
about today's women

The compelling thrill
of romantic excitement

It could happen to you!

EXPERIENCE
HARLEQUIN ROMANCE!

Available wherever Harlequin books are sold.

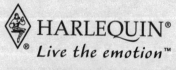

HARLEQUIN®
Live the emotion™

www.eHarlequin.com

HROMDIR09

HARLEQUIN®

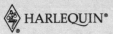

American ★ Romance®

Invites *you* to experience lively, heartwarming all-American romances

Every month, we bring you four strong, sexy men, and four women who know what they want—and go all out to get it.

From small towns to big cities, experience a sense of adventure, romance and family spirit—the all-American way!

American ★ Romance®

Love, Home & Happiness

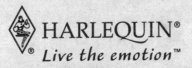

HARLEQUIN®
Live the emotion™

www.eHarlequin.com   HARDIR09

HARLEQUIN®
INTRIGUE®

BREATHTAKING ROMANTIC SUSPENSE

Shared dangers and passions lead to electrifying romance and heart-stopping suspense!

Every month, you'll meet six new heroes who are guaranteed to make your spine tingle and your pulse pound. With them you'll enter into the exciting world of Harlequin Intrigue— where your life is on the line and so is your heart!

THAT'S INTRIGUE—
ROMANTIC SUSPENSE
AT ITS BEST!

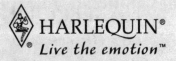

HARLEQUIN®
Live the emotion™

www.eHarlequin.com   INTDIR06

HARLEQUIN®

Super Romance®

...there's more to the story!

Superromance.
A *big* satisfying read about unforgettable characters. Each month we offer *six* very different stories that range from family drama to adventure and mystery, from highly emotional stories to romantic comedies—and much more! Stories about people you'll believe in and care about. Stories too compelling to put down....

Our authors are among today's *best* romance writers. You'll find familiar names and talented newcomers. Many of them are award winners— and you'll see why!

If you want the biggest and best in romance fiction, you'll get it from Superromance!

Exciting, Emotional, Unexpected...

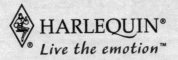

HARLEQUIN®
Live the emotion™

www.eHarlequin.com   HSDIR06

Harlequin® Historical
Historical Romantic Adventure!

*Imagine a time of chivalrous
knights and unconventional ladies,
roguish rakes and impetuous
heiresses, rugged cowboys
and spirited frontierswomen—
these rich and vivid tales will
capture your imagination!*

*Harlequin Historical...
they're too good to miss!*

HHDIR06